Teacher's Edition

Jazz Chant
FAIRY TALES

CAROLYN GRAHAM

Jazz Chant FAIRY TALES

CAROLYN GRAHAM

Illustrators
Mimi Brennan
Marybeth Farrell
John O'Brien

Oxford University Press
1988

Oxford University Press

200 Madison Avenue
New York, NY 10016 USA

Walton Street
Oxford OX2 6DP England

OXFORD is a trademark of Oxford University Press.

ISBN 0-19-434300-6

Developmental Editor: Debbie Sistino
Associate Editor: Lisa Ahlquist
Art Director: Shireen Nathoo
Arts Researcher: Paula Radding
Senior Designer: Mark Kellogg

Printing (last digit): 9 8 7 6 5 4 3 2 1
Printed in the United States of America.

TABLE OF CONTENTS   Page

WHAT IS A JAZZ CHANT?

A jazz chant is the rhythmic expression of standard American English. Jazz chants are designed to teach the natural rhythm, stress, and intonation patterns of conversational American English.

Just as the selection of a particular tempo and beat in jazz may convey powerful and varied emotions, the rhythm, stress, and intonation patterns of the spoken language are essential elements for the expression of feelings and the intent of the speaker. Linking these two dynamic forms has produced an innovative and exciting approach to language learning.

Although jazz chanting's primary purpose is the improvement of speaking and listening comprehension skills, it also works well in reinforcing specific grammar and pronunciation patterns.

WHAT IS A JAZZ CHANT FAIRY TALE?

A Jazz Chant Fairy Tale is a fairy tale that has been rewritten as a performance piece for children emphasizing rhythm and rhyme. Each fairy tale has a strong rhythmic underpinning, occasionally broken by a passage where the narrator or other solo voices speak in a simple conversational style without accompaniment.

The fairy tales selected for this book are all internationally known and many will already be familiar to young children. Each fairy tale contains a number of roles, both solo and choral, providing an opportunity for every child to participate in class, and ultimately in the final production.

GENERAL NOTES

General suggestions for presenting the fairy tales are listed below. It should be noted that these are simply suggestions, and you should feel free to experiment and improvise to meet the needs of your own students.

Step 1   With books closed, slowly tell the students the fairy tale in your own words. Use whatever repetitions and explanations necessary to be certain that all of the students have a clear understanding of the characters and conflicts presented in each fairy tale. If you prefer, you may want to simply read the narrative version of the fairy tales included in the teacher's notes.

Step 2   With books still closed, play the cassette and have students listen to the fairy tale.

Step 3   Have students listen to the fairy tale on the cassette again and follow along with books open. Students should not speak during this step.

Step 4   Have students do a line-by-line choral reading of the fairy tale. Provide a model and have the students repeat after you with books open.

Step 5   Play the cassette again. Students listen and read along only with the chorus. Books are open.

Step 6   Assign roles and do a complete drama reading. Practice and repeat lines as necessary for correct rhythm and intonation.

Step 7   Assign roles to students to practice and memorize at home.

Step 8   Rehearse the fairy tale and perform it in class.

Step 9   Prepare for a performance in school assembly.

Beginning-level students will obviously need more repetition and teacher modeling. You may wish to slow down the tempo, but be careful to retain the same stress and intonation pattern.

Advanced-level students may want to take these performance pieces one step farther and write their own fairy tales or plays to perform for the class or school.

PAIR PRACTICE AND RETELLING THE STORY

The pair practice and retelling the story activities provided in the teacher's notes are designed to offer extra speaking and listening comprehension practice. The pair practice usually focuses on one or two specific pronunciation or grammar points. The pair practice activities could be accompanied by clapping or "patty cake" routines. This helps reinforce the rhythm and tempo.

Retelling the story provides students with a listening and speaking activity to be performed after they are thoroughly familiar with the fairy tale. Each statement in the retelling the story activity is written with an untrue element. For example, in the statement *Once upon a time there were* four *bears,* students would substitute the word *three* for *four.* With books closed, read each statement to the class and have students make the corrections by supplying the true information.

BACKGROUND RHYTHM

When practicing a Jazz Chant Fairy Tale, establish a strong, clear rhythm by counting and clapping (one clap, two clap, three clap, four clap). Choose a tempo that is comfortable for the students and slowly increase in speed until you are following the tempo presented on the cassette. You may wish to use a mechanical device such as a metronome, Casio keyboard, or drum machine to keep the rhythm going.

Another way to establish rhythm is to form a student rhythm band. The band members could play simple homemade instruments such as rhythm sticks, wood blocks, gourds, or soda cans filled with pebbles. Students in the band could choose a name and create costumes following the theme of the story. For example, they might want to dress as butterflies and flowers while accompanying *The Three Billy Goats Gruff.*

CASTING

Each fairy tale has a narrator, several major roles, and a chorus so that all students can participate in each performance. All roles should be open to all students despite language level or appearance. Since theater is make-believe, a student can pretend to be anything including a fish, bear, boy, or girl.

PERFORMANCE

If you are presenting one of the fairy tales to an audience, you may want to pass out copies of the script and have them participate as members of the chorus while the students take the solo roles. One student should be assigned the role of chorus director and would be responsible for directing the audience chorus and on-stage student activity.

COSTUMES   Students may wish to design and create simple headbands or masks to wear during their performance. For example, Goldilocks could make a headband adorned with long curls of yellow construction paper, and the bears could have headbands with brown bear ears. The members of the chorus may also wear special headbands. In *The Fisherman and His Wife,* the chorus members could divide into various kinds of sea creatures such as dolphins, sharks, or mermaids and create headbands to represent those characters.

If your students are really motivated, they can create a simple set in addition to costumes.

STRUCTURE KEY

GOLDILOCKS AND THE THREE BEARS

SUMMARY

Once upon a time there were three bears who lived in a little house in the woods. One morning while they were getting ready for breakfast, the three bears decided to let their porridge cool and go for a walk.

While they were gone, a little girl with long, golden hair was walking through the woods and saw the bears' house. Everybody called her Goldilocks because her hair was the color of gold. Goldilocks walked up to the front door and knocked, but nobody answered. She peeked into the windows, but she didn't see anybody. She knocked again, but still nobody came to the door

Finally, she decided to go inside the little house and look around. She looked in the kitchen and saw the breakfast table set for three. There were three chairs and three bowls of nice porridge. Goldilocks was very hungry and decided to try some of the porridge. First she sat down in Papa Bear's chair, but it was too big and his porridge was too hot. Then she sat down in Mama Bear's chair, but it was too hard and her porridge was too cold. Finally, she sat down in Baby Bear's chair and it was just right. The porridge was so delicious that she ate it all up. She was having a wonderful time when all of a sudden, the chair fell apart and Goldilocks fell to the floor.

Goldilocks felt very sorry about the broken chair, but she also felt sleepy. So she decided to take a nap. She walked to the bedroom and saw three beds. First she tried Papa Bear's bed, but it was too big. Then she tried Mama Bear's bed, but it was too hard. Finally, she tried Baby Bear's bed, and it was just right. She climbed right in and fell fast asleep.

Just then, the bears came home. They were shocked and upset when they saw that someone had been in their house, eating their porridge and sitting in their chairs. Baby Bear was very upset when he saw that his little chair was broken and his porridge bowl was empty.

When the bears looked into their bedroom, Papa Bear and Mama Bear were both surprised to find that someone had been sleeping in their beds, but Baby Bear had the biggest surprise of all. There was little Goldilocks, asleep in his bed. Baby Bear shouted for his mama and papa. Just then, Goldilocks woke up, took one look at the three bears, and jumped out the window. She ran into the woods, and no one ever saw her again.

STRUCTURE NOTES   This fairy tale offers practice with:

Plurals: Listen to the /z/ sound of the plural *s* in bears, bowls, spoons, napkins, and chairs. Listen to the /ez/ sound of *es* in glasses.

Possessive S: Papa Bear's, Mama Bear's, and Baby Bear's. The plural possessive looks like this: bears'.

Past Tense Irregular Forms: were, set, made, sat, left, felt, began, heard, was, saw, fell, ate, drank, been, put, came, broke, woke, ran, and gone.

Past Continuous Tense: *She was having a wonderful time* and *Someone's been sitting in my chair*. The past continuous tense refers to an action that happened in the past and is used to describe a scene when telling a story.

Question Words: how many, who, where, and what.

Exclamations: *Ow, wow! Oh, no! Someone's been sleeping in my bed! Here she is! Well, that's that!*

Contractions: where's, that's, what's, who's, anybody's, and there's. They indicate a combination of word + is. Notice the contraction I'll (I will) to indicate the future and wasn't (was not) to indicate the negative.

PAIR PRACTICE   This exercise offers practice with the question words *what* and *how many.*

A: Once upon a time there were three bears.
B: Three what?
A: Three bears.

B: Once upon a time there were three bears.
A: How many bears?
B: Three.

This exercise emphasizes the question word *who* and the third person *s* in *loves.*

A: Who loves Mama?
B: Papa loves Mama.
A: Who loves Papa?
B: Mama loves Papa.

(**PAIR PRACTICE** continued on next page)

PAIR PRACTICE	This exercise emphasizes information questions.

A: Who set the table?
B: Baby set the table.
A: Who poured the milk?
B: Mama poured the milk.
A: Who made the porridge?
B: Papa made the porridge.

This exercise offers practice with *what* and *who* in the contracted form.

A: What's that? Who's there?
B: What's that? Who's there?
A: What's that? Who's there?
B: I hope it's a bear.

RETELLING THE STORY	Write these sentences on the board or read them out loud. Ask your students to correct the statements.

1. Once upon a time there were <u>four</u> bears.

2. Goldilocks was a little girl with long, <u>black</u> hair.

3. Mama Bear <u>didn't like</u> Papa Bear.

4. The bears went for a walk because their porridge was very <u>cold</u>.

5. Goldilocks ate all of <u>Mama Bear's</u> porridge.

6. The Bear family lived in <u>an apartment in the city</u>.

7. Goldilocks <u>wasn't</u> very sleepy after eating all the porridge.

8. When Goldilocks woke up and saw the three bears, she <u>smiled and went right back to sleep</u>.

LITTLE RED RIDING HOOD

SUMMARY   Once upon a time there was a good girl called Little Red Riding Hood. One morning her mother baked some cookies and asked Little Red Riding Hood to take them to her grandmother. Granny was home alone and sick in bed, in a little house in the woods.

Little Red Riding Hood's mother told her to be very careful. She warned her not to talk to strangers and not to stop for anything along the way to Granny's house. Little Red Riding Hood promised her mother that she would be very careful. She picked up the cookies and started off for Granny's house.

On the way, Little Red Riding Hood met a big bad wolf who pretended to be very friendly. He asked Little Red Riding Hood a lot of questions about who she was and where she was going. She forgot everything her mother had said and told the wolf all about her granny who was home alone and sick in bed. The wolf suggested she stop for awhile and pick some flowers for her granny. That sounded like a wonderful idea to Little Red Riding Hood. While she was picking the flowers, the big bad wolf disappeared into the woods.

He ran straight to Granny's house and found her alone and sick in bed. The big bad wolf gobbled her up in one big bite. Then he went to the closet, put on some of Granny's clothes, and climbed into bed to wait for Little Red Riding Hood.

Soon, the wolf heard Little Red Riding Hood's knock at the door. Pretending to be Granny, he invited her into the bedroom. When she saw the wolf in bed, she thought it was Granny but she thought her Granny looked awfully strange. "Oh, Granny! What big ears you have," she said. "The better to hear you with," said the wolf. "And Granny, what big eyes you have," she said. "The better to see you with," said the wolf. "And Granny, what big teeth you have," said Little Red Riding Hood. "The better to eat you with," said the wolf.

He jumped out of bed, grabbed Little Red Riding Hood and ate her up in one big bite. The wolf became so sleepy after eating so much that he lay down on the bed, fell asleep, and began to snore. The sound of his snoring was so loud that a friendly hunter walking by the house heard the noise and stopped to see if Granny was all right. When he discovered the wolf asleep in Granny's bed, he realized what had happened. The friendly hunter took a big pair of scissors and cut the wolf's stomach open. To his surprise, out popped Little Red Riding Hood followed by Granny. They quickly gathered stones and put them in the wolf's stomach.

When the wolf woke up, he had such a stomachache that he fell right down and died. Granny, Little Red Riding Hood, and the friendly hunter were safe and everyone lived happily ever after.

STRUCTURE NOTES   This fairy tale offers practice with:

Plurals: Listen to the /z/ sound of the plural s in cookies, strangers, clothes, arms, ears, eyes, woods, things, flowers, covers, stories, girls, and grannies. Listen to the /s/ sound of the plural in moments.

Notice the irregular plural of tooth: teeth.

Possessive S: mother's, Granny's, and wolf's.

Present Tense Third Person -S: smells, says, and lives.

Past Tense Irregular Forms: did, made, wore, was, went, sat, woke, took, came, forgot, spoke, thought, ran, heard, saw, fell, and died.

Past Continuous Tense: *One morning Little Red Riding Hood was sleeping. She woke up when she heard her mother's voice.* The past continuous tense refers to an action that happened in the past and is used to describe a scene when telling a story.

Question Words: how, what's, where, who, and why.

Imperative Statements: *Go straight to Granny's house. Don't stop along the way. Be a good little girl.* Imperative statements are usually commands that do not have a stated subject but the implied subject you.

Time Expressions: *All of the time* and *always* indicate an action that always takes place. *Most of the time* indicates an action that sometimes takes place.

The following are vocabulary and expressions you might want to explain to your class: sick in bed, gobbled up, one big bite, and fast asleep.

PAIR PRACTICE
This exercise focuses on the verb in the infinitive and the past tense forms.

A: When Mama said "Go," she went.
B: When Mama said "Stay," she stayed.
A: When Mama said "Sit," she sat.
B: When Mama said "Play," she played.

This exercise offers practice with asking and answering yes/no questions.

A: Was she good?
B: Yes, she was.
A: Was she very good?
B: Yes, she was.
A: Did she listen to her mother?
B: Yes, she did.
A: All of the time?
B: Most of the time.

This exercise also emphasizes asking and answering yes/no questions. Notice the rising intonation of the question.

A: Is the wolf dead?
B: Yes, he is.
A: Are you sure he's dead?
B: Yes, I am.
A: Is your Granny OK?
B: Yes, she is.
A: Are you sure she's OK?
B: Yes, I am.

This exercise offers practice with imperative statements.

A: Go straight to Granny's house.
B: Yes, Mama I will.
A: Don't stop along the way.
B: No, Mama I won't.
A: Be a good little girl.
B: Yes, Mama I will.
A: Don't talk to strangers.
B: No, Mama I won't.

RETELLING THE STORY
Write these sentences on the board or read them out loud. Ask your students to correct the statements.

1. Once upon a time there was a <u>bad</u> little girl called Little Red Riding Hood.

2. When she was on her way to Granny's house she met a <u>huge dog</u>.

3. She went straight to Granny's house and <u>didn't stop for anything</u>.

(**RETELLING THE STORY** continued on next page)

4. When the wolf spoke to her, <u>she didn't answer</u>.

5. She <u>didn't tell</u> the wolf where Granny lived.

6. Little Red Riding Hood's mother made <u>ginger</u> cookies.

7. <u>Granny ate the wolf</u> up in one big bite.

8. A friendly <u>woodchopper</u> was walking along in the woods and heard the wolf snoring.

9. Granny and Little Red Riding Hood put <u>feathers</u> in the wolf's stomach to make him heavy.

10. When the wolf woke up, he had a terrible <u>headache</u> and fell right down and died.

CHICKEN LITTLE

SUMMARY   One morning Chicken Little was walking along the road when a small acorn fell, and landed right on her head. She was surprised and very scared because she thought it was a piece of the sky. She was sure the sky was falling in. She began to hurry down the road to the King's palace to tell him the terrible news.

On the way, she met her old friend, Henny Penny. When Chicken Little told her that the sky was falling in, Henny Penny was surprised and scared too. So Henny Penny and Chicken Little hurried together down the road to the King's palace. Soon they met their old friend Cocky Locky. They told him what the problem was immediately. When he heard that the sky was falling in, Cocky Locky wanted to come with them. So the three friends hurried quickly down the road to the King's castle. Pretty soon they met their friend Ducky Wucky. As soon as they told him that the sky was falling in, he was just as scared as they were and wanted to come with them to tell the King the terrible news.

Now Chicken Little, Henny Penny, Cocky Locky, and Ducky Wucky all hurried down the road and soon they met their old friend Goosey Woosey. They told him immediately about the sky falling in. As soon as he heard the news, he wanted to come with them. So now Chicken Little, Henny Penny, Cocky Locky, Ducky Wucky, and Goosey Woosey all hurried together down the road to the King's castle.

As they were hurrying along the road, just as fast as they could go, they ran right into their old friend Turkey Lurkey. He was surprised to see all of his friends running along the road, but when they told him the terrible news about the sky falling in, he was even more surprised. Turkey Lurkey decided to join them right away.

Now they were all hurrying along the road when suddenly they met Foxy Woxy. Foxy Woxy was very surprised to see all those wonderful animals running along the road. He asked Chicken Little and her friends where they were going. They didn't have time to stop, but as they were running along, they told Foxy Woxy the story of the sky falling in and explained that they had to tell the King.

Now Foxy Woxy was a clever fellow. He didn't believe for a minute that the sky was really falling in, but he knew that Chicken Little and her friends would make a wonderful Sunday dinner. So he pretended to be just as surprised and scared as they were and said, "Come follow me. I'll take you to the King." So Chicken Little, Henny Penny, Cocky Locky, Ducky Wucky, Goosey Woosey, and Turkey Lurkey all followed Foxy Woxy and nobody ever saw them again. And nobody told the King.

STRUCTURE NOTES   This fairy tale offers practice with:

Past Tense Irregular Forms: woke, was, began, met, did, thought, hurried, said, fell, told, went, heard, and saw.

Present Continuous Tense: *The sky is falling in. Where are you going?* The present continuous tense refers to action that is occuring at the moment.

Past Continuous Tense: *The sun was shining.* The past continuous tense refers to an action that happened in the past and is used to describe a scene when telling a story.

Future, Be Going To: *What are you going to tell the King? We're going to see the King.* This future tense describes intentions.

Modals: *Must, have to,* and *has to* express necessity. *Can't* expresses inability.

Possessive S: the King's castle.

Question Words: what, where, who, how, and why.

Contractions: Word + is/are: what's, that's, we're, and you're. Notice the contractions what'll, I'll, and he'll (word + will) to indicate the future. Notice the contractions can't, don't, haven't, and didn't (word + not) to indicate the negative.

PAIR PRACTICE   This exercise offers practice with asking and answering questions.

A: What did you say?
B: The sky is falling in.
A: What fell?
B: A piece of the sky.
A: That's what I thought you said.

This exercise also emphasizes asking and answering questions.

A: What fell?
B: A piece of the sky.
A: When did it fall?
B: A minute ago.

PAIR PRACTICE

This exercise offers practice with the question word *what* and the modals *can't* and *have to.*

A: What's your hurry? Slow down.
B: I can't slow down. I have to tell the King.
A: What's the matter? What's wrong?
B: The sky is falling in.

This exercise offers practice with the question word *how.*

A: Cocky Locky, how do you know?
B: Henny Penny told me so.
A: Henny Penny, how do you know?
B: Chicken Little told me so.

This exercise offers practice with the modals *must* and *have to.*

A: I must see the King.
B: Why do you want to do that?
A: I have to see the King.
B: Why do you have to see the King?
A: The sky is falling in.

RETELLING THE STORY

Write these sentences on the board or read them out loud. Ask your students to correct the statements.

1. One morning when Chicken Little was walking along the road, a big flower fell on her head.

2. She thought it was a raindrop.

3. She said, "Oh, no! It's raining. I must tell my mother."

4. When she told her good friend Henny Penny that the sky was falling in, Henny Penny just laughed and said, "Don't be silly."

5. Chicken Little only met two friends on her way to see the King.

6. Foxy Woxy was not a very smart fellow.

THE THREE BILLY GOATS GRUFF

SUMMARY
Once upon a time there were three Billy Goats Gruff. Their names were Big Bill, Will, and Little Billy. One day they decided to visit their favorite hill and look for something good to eat. Before they could get to the hill, they had to cross a bridge. Under the bridge lived a mean, ugly troll. The troll liked to fight and bite and slap and kick, and he especially liked to eat anything, including goats.

Soon the three Billy Goats Gruff came to the bridge. Little Billy was the first to cross. The troll heard the pitter pat of Little Billy's feet and shouted, ''Who's there? What's that?'' The troll threatened to eat the little goat up, but Little Billy said, ''Oh, no. Don't eat me. I'm too small, but you'll like my brother Will. He's much bigger and fatter.''

The troll let Little Billy cross the bridge and waited for Will to come along. Soon the troll heard the rat-a-tat-tat of Will's feet and shouted, ''Who's there? What's that?'' The troll threatened to eat the goat up, but Will said, ''Oh, no. You don't want me. You should wait and see my big, fat brother Bill. You'll just love him.''

The troll let Will cross the bridge and waited for Big Bill to come along. Soon the troll heard the clump, clump, clump of Big Bill's feet and shouted, ''Who's there? What's that?'' The troll looked up at Big Bill and saw that he was big and fat. He was perfect for dinner. Big Bill answered the troll and then asked him to come up on the bridge. Big Bill told the troll that goats were smarter than trolls, and the troll got very angry. As they were arguing, Big Bill kept asking the troll to take a little step closer to him so he could hear better. Soon, when the troll got near the edge of the bridge, Big Bill gave him a big push and the troll fell down into the water. The three Billy Goats Gruff were able to cross the bridge and eat at their favorite hill, and nobody ever saw the troll again.

STRUCTURE NOTES
This fairy tale offers practice with:

Plurals: Listen to the /z/ sound of the plural s in butterflies, daisies, dandelions, lambs, tin cans, golf balls, brothers, and trolls. Listen to the /s/ sound of the plural in goats, pancakes, carrot tops, and milk shakes.

Possessive S: Big Bill's brother.

Present Tense Third Person -S: likes, eats, calls, and comes.

STRUCTURE NOTES	**Comparatives:** *bigger, fatter, smarter,* and *closer.* Comparisons using as or like are also highlighted: *not as big as, fat as a pig, he sank like a stone.*
	Superlatives: the best and the oldest.
	Past Tense Irregular Forms: was, did, began, had, heard, went, made, said, thought, gave, fell, sank, and saw.
	Future, Be Going To: *I'm going to. . . .* This tense demonstrates the intention of an action.
	Modals: *ought* to express possibility: *You ought to meet my brother Will.*
	Exclamations: *Hey! Watch out! Not that!*
	Contractions: I'm (word + be) and he's, Billy's, Will's, who's, and what's (word + is). Notice the contractions I'll and he'll (word + will) to indicate the future and didn't and wasn't (word + not) to indicate the negative.

PAIR PRACTICE	This exercise offers practice with *like to* and exclamations.

A: I like to fight and bite!
B: I like to kick and slap!
A: I like to pinch and punch!
B: I like to push and shove!
A: Fight and bite and kick and slap!
B: Pinch and punch and push and shove!

This exercise offers practice with the contraction *I'll* and the plural *s.*

A: I'll eat anything, anything at all.
B: Tin cans?
A: Anything!
B: Pancakes?
A: Anything!
B: Carrot tops?
A: Anything, anything at all!

This exercise offers practice with exclamations.

A: Watch out for the troll, watch out, watch out!
B: The troll eats goats, watch out!
A: Watch out for the troll, he'll eat you up!
B: He'll eat you up, watch out!

RETELLING THE STORY

Write these sentences on the board or read them out loud. Ask your students to correct the statements.

1. Once upon a time, there were <u>two</u> Billy Goats Gruff.
2. The youngest Billy Goat's name was <u>Little Bobby</u>.
3. Big Bill <u>didn't like</u> to eat anything.
4. When Little Billy tried to cross the bridge, the terrible troll <u>ate him up</u>.
5. Will said that <u>Little Billy</u> was the biggest and fattest goat of all.
6. The <u>troll</u> pushed <u>Big Bill</u> off the bridge.

THE THREE LITTLE PIGS

SUMMARY

Once upon a time there were three little pigs who lived together with their father and their mother. One morning Mother Pig called her three sons and said that it was time for them to leave home and go out into the big world alone. Before they left, she warned her sons to never let a wolf in their door.

And so the three little pigs left home. As they walked, the road soon split into three directions. Big Brother Pig said that each of them must choose a direction. He warned his brothers again about the wolf and then chose the road on the left. Brother Pig chose the road on the right, and Baby Pig skipped happily down the middle road.

On his way down the road, Baby Pig met a man carrying straw. Baby Pig bought three bundles of the straw to build a house to keep him safe from the wolf. He quickly built his house of straw. It wasn't very pretty and it wasn't very good, but he loved it. Baby Pig soon went to sleep. Suddenly, he heard a loud knock. "Who's there?" cried Baby Pig. The wolf answered, "A friend." Baby Pig knew it was a wolf and didn't let him in, but the wolf huffed and puffed and blew Baby Pig's house down. Then he ate Baby Pig up in one big bite.

While all this was happening, Brother Pig was walking down the road when he met the man selling straw. "I want something stronger than straw," said Brother Pig. So he continued down the road until he met a man selling sticks. "I'm going to build my house of sticks," said Brother Pig. "Sticks are stronger than straw."

Brother Pig bought the sticks and worked hard all day long building his house. When he was finished, he went inside, locked the door, and went to sleep. Suddenly, there was a loud knock. "What's that?" cried Brother Pig. "Your brother," answered the wolf. Brother Pig knew that it was not his brother, and would not let the wolf in. But the wolf huffed and puffed and blew Brother Pig's house down and ate him up in one big bite.

While all this was happening, Big Brother Pig met the man selling straw as he walked down his road. Big Brother Pig wanted something stronger than straw to build a house. So he continued down the road and then met the man selling sticks. Big Brother Pig wanted something stronger than sticks to build a house. Again, he continued down the road when he met a man selling bricks. "I'm going to build my house of bricks," said Big Brother Pig. "Bricks are stronger than sticks and straw."

So Big Brother Pig bought the bricks and carefully built his house. When he was finished, he went inside, locked the door, and hung a large cooking pot over the fire in the fireplace. The water in the pot was boiling when suddenly he heard a loud knock on the door. "What's that? Who's there?" cried Big Brother Pig. "Open the door and you will see who I am," answered the wolf. Big Brother Pig would not let the wolf in.

(**SUMMARY** continued on next page)

SUMMARY

So the wolf huffed and puffed, but the house did not blow down. The wolf was getting very angry. He shouted that he was coming down the chimney. ''Good idea,'' cried Big Brother Pig.

So the wolf jumped down the chimney and fell right into the big pot of boiling water. And that was the end of the big bad wolf and the story of the three little pigs.

STRUCTURE NOTES

This fairy tale offers practice with:

Plurals: Notice the /z/ sound of the plural s in pigs, boys, directions, brothers, sons, bundles, roads, and babies. Notice the /s/ sound of the plural in sticks, and bricks.

Possessive S: Baby Pig's brother.

Past Tense Irregular Forms: said, taught, left, told, was, met, bought, began, stood, went, blew, ate, fell, built, hung, tried, and came.

Past Continuous and Simple Past: *Baby Pig was skipping when he met, Brother Pig was walking . . . and he too met, the water was boiling when suddenly he heard,* and *the wolf was getting angry and finally he threatened.* The past continuous tense is used for an action that was going on in the past and the simple past tense is used for an action that interrupted what was going on.

Past Perfect Tense: *had taught* and *had built.* The past perfect tense describes an action that took place before another past action.

Future, Will: *I'll huff, I'll puff, I'll blow your house down,* and *I'll explain it later.*

Future, Be Going To: *I'm going to build my house of bricks.* This future tense describes intentions.

Comparatives: older and stronger.

Imperative Statements: *Never let a wolf in your door. Open the door. Let me in. Go away. Go ahead. Try it. Come right in.* Imperative statements are usually commands that do not have a stated subject but the implied subject you.

| **PAIR PRACTICE** | This exercise offers practice with contractions and the possessive *s*. |

A: What's that? Who's there?
B: Your brother.
A: That's not my brother's voice. Who's there?
B: Open the door. Let me in.
A: Not by the hair of my chinny chin chin.

This exercise offers practice with the comparative form *stronger*.

A: Straw for sale.
   Straw for sale.
   Clean, fresh straw.
B: I want something stronger than straw,
   much stronger than straw.
A: Sticks for sale.
   Sticks for sale.
   Good, hard sticks for sale.
B: I want something stronger than sticks,
   much stronger than sticks.

This exercise offers practice with the contraction *I'll*.

A: Open the door. Let me in.
B: Not by the hair of my chinny chin chin.
A: Then I'll huff and I'll puff and I'll blow your house down.
B: Go ahead. Try it.

RETELLING THE STORY

Write the sentences on the board or read them out loud. Ask your students to correct the statements.

1. Once upon a time there were <u>two</u> little pigs.

2. Their mother told them the wolf was a <u>very friendly fellow</u>.

3. She told them <u>to invite the wolf into their house</u>.

4. A straw house <u>is very strong</u>.

5. Straw is <u>stronger</u> than sticks.

6. The brick house <u>fell down</u> as soon as the wolf began to huff and puff.

7. Big Brother Pig built his house very <u>quickly and carelessly</u>.

8. The big bad wolf jumped down the chimney and fell right into <u>a nice soft bed</u>.

LITTLE RED HEN

SUMMARY

Once upon a time, there was a Little Red Hen who worked very hard everyday. She scratched in the barnyard from morning until night looking for something to eat. The Little Red Hen was not alone in the barnyard. There was a lazy dog who was always tired. There was a crazy cat who went, ''Meow, meow, meow.'' And there was a duck who went, ''Quack.'' The dog, the cat, and the duck sat around the barnyard all day long and watched the Little Red Hen work and scratch.

One day, the Little Red Hen found some grains of wheat. She was very happy and decided to plant them. She asked the dog, the cat, and the duck if they would help her, but they all said no. So the Little Red Hen had to plant the grains of wheat all by herself.

The wheat grew and grew, and soon it was tall and strong and ready to cut. The Little Red Hen asked the others if they would help her cut the wheat. They all said no. They were too busy doing nothing to help. So again, the Little Red Hen had to do the job all by herself.

When she had finished cutting the wheat, she had to take it to the mill to be ground into flour. The Little Red Hen asked if anyone would help, but they all said no. So she took the wheat to the mill all by herself.

When she came back from the mill with the flour, she was ready to make bread. She asked if anyone would help her. Again, nobody helped her at all and the Little Red Hen had to do the work alone.

At last, the fresh, warm bread was ready and the dog and the cat and the duck gathered around the Little Red Hen hoping for a nice big piece. ''Oh, no!'' said the Little Red Hen. ''Nobody helped. Nobody will eat. I'm going to eat this bread all by myself!'' And she did.

STRUCTURE NOTES

This fairy tale offers practice with:

Plurals: Notice the /z/ sound of the plural s in chickens, grains, and roosters. Notice the /s/ sound of the plural in chicks.

Past Tense Irregular Forms: was, went, found, did, grew, cut, carried, and ground.

Question Words: what, where, why, and who.

Modals: *have to* and *can't*. These modals express necessity and impossibility.

Future, Will: *What'll you do? Will you? Who will help me? I'll have to do it myself. I will. So will I.*

Definite and Indefinite Articles: The *a/the* distinction is found in *a cat in the yard* and *a dog in the yard.*

Polite Refusals: *I'm afraid I can't. I wish I could, but I'm afraid I can't. I'm sorry, I can't.*

PAIR PRACTICE

This exercise offers practice with question words and polite refusals.

A: Who will help me cut the wheat?
B: Not me.
A: Why not?
B: I can't.
A: Why not?
B: I wish I could, but I'm afraid I can't.

This exercise also emphasizes practice with polite refusals.

A: Who will help me bake the bread?
B: Bake the bread? I'm sorry I can't.
A: Oh well, I'll have to do it myself.

This exercise offers practice with the future *will.*

A: Who will help me eat this bread?
B: I will.
A: Oh, no you won't.
B: Oh, yes I will.
A: Oh, no you won't.
B: I will.
A: You won't.
B: I will.
A: You won't.
B: Why not?
A: Because I'll eat it myself.

RETELLING THE STORY

Write these sentences on the board or read them out loud. Ask your students to correct the statements.

1. Once upon a time there was a <u>big brown</u> hen.

2. She was <u>very lazy</u>.

3. There was a dog in the yard that went, "<u>Quack, quack, quack.</u>"

4. The dog <u>worked very hard</u>.

5. The hen found some grains of <u>corn</u> in the barnyard.

6. The dog, cat, and duck <u>were very happy to help</u> the hen.

7. After the wheat was cut, the Little Red Hen brought it to the <u>garage</u> to be ground.

8. The Little Red Hen <u>shared her bread with everyone</u>.

RUMPELSTILTSKIN

SUMMARY

Once upon a time, there was a poor working man who had a very pretty and smart daughter. He thought his daughter was the most wonderful girl in the world. In fact, he used to say his daughter could do anything, even spin straw into gold.

One day the King heard that there was a girl in his kingdom who could spin straw into gold. He sent for her father immediately and asked if this was really true. The father said the girl really could spin straw into gold and agreed to bring her to the King.

So the father went home and told his daughter that the King wanted to meet her and listen to her sing. The daughter asked, "How can I sing for the King?" The father answered, "Just go, my dear, and sing for the King." When the daughter met the King, she was confused. She thought she was going to sing, but he wanted her to spin. She looked to her father and asked him to explain that she could not spin straw into gold. The father answered, "Do the best you can, my child."

The King took the girl to a small dark room. She looked around and saw nothing but straw and a spinning wheel. The King said that if she couldn't turn the straw into gold, she would die. "What am I going to do?" said the girl. "Oh, someone, somewhere, help me please." And she began to cry.

Soon a little man dressed in silver walked through the door. He asked her what was wrong and she told him her problem. The little man said he could help her if she gave him something. The girl gave the man her necklace and he began to spin. The sound of the spinning wheel was so sweet, she fell asleep and didn't wake up until the next morning. When she opened her eyes, the little man was gone and the room was full of gold.

When the King came in, he was so pleased that he put the girl in a larger room filled with straw, and told her to do it again. She looked around at the piles of straw, sat down, and began to cry. Soon, the man dressed in silver came and said he could help her if she gave him something. The girl gave the man her ring and he began to spin. The sound of the spinning wheel was so sweet, she fell asleep and didn't wake up until the next morning. When she opened her eyes, the man was gone and the room was full of gold.

When the King came in, he was so pleased that he put the girl in an even larger room filled with straw and told her to do it again. This time he promised to make her Queen if she could spin all the straw into gold. Once the King left, the girl called to her little friend. "Come back, come back, wherever you are. I need you now. Come back!" she cried.

Soon he came through the door. The girl told him that if he could spin the straw into gold one more time, she would be Queen. The little man said he would, but he wanted something in return. The girl had nothing left to give him, but promised

SUMMARY her firstborn child in return for spinning the straw into gold. For the third time, the tiny man sat down and began to spin. The sound of the wheel was so sweet, she fell asleep. When she woke up, the King was standing near her, and the room was full of gold.

"Wake up, my dear. You're going to be Queen," the King said. And so the girl married the King, and soon forgot all about her terrible promise. After a year, they had a beautiful daughter. Then one day when the Queen was in the nursery, the door opened. It was the little man. He had come for the child.

The Queen became very upset and asked the little man if he would like something else instead of the child. He said no, but gave the Queen three days to guess his name. If she didn't guess his name, the child would be his. The Queen thought for a whole day about the little man's name. On the second day, the little man returned and gave her a clue. He told her that his name started with R.

At the end of the second day, the Queen sent her messengers all over the land to search for clues to the name. On the afternoon of the third day, one of her messengers came running into the palace. He told the Queen that he saw the little man dancing around a fire singing "Rumpelstiltskin."

When the little man returned to the palace at the end of the third day, he asked the Queen if she had guessed his name. The queen replied, "Rumpelstiltskin." Rumpelstiltskin screamed, "Oh, no! I lost the game! Yes, Rumpelstiltskin is my name." And with these words, Rumpelstiltskin began to spin around. He fell to the ground in a cloud of silver smoke. Only a tiny silver button remained. The King and Queen lived happily ever after, and the little daughter loved to listen to her mother tell her favorite story—the story of Rumpelstiltskin.

STRUCTURE NOTES   This fairy tale offers practice with:

Plurals: Notice the /z/ sound of the plural s in shoes, diamonds, pearls, days, messengers, clues, things, stockings, piles, names, and words.

Past Tense Irregular Forms: was, thought, did, heard, sent, went, told, took, saw, sat, began, spoke, fell, gone, knew, left, married, forgot, had, came, sent, found, hurried, hid, gave, won, and lost.

Past Continuous Tense: *He was there bouncing around the room, a fire was burning,* and *a man was dancing.* The past continuous tense describes a continuous action that was going on in the past.

Present Perfect Tense: *I have heard* and *I've never seen such a thing in my life!* The present perfect tense is used here to describe vague, indefinite past time.

Future, Will: *You will die, what will you do for me, I'll make you my wife, I'll be Queen, what will I get, I will take your firstborn child,* and *you'll have my child.*

If-Clauses: *I must see for myself if she can spin straw into gold. If you can't, you will die. If you only knew.*

Present Tense Third Person -S: wants, spins, and starts.

Superlatives: most beautiful, smartest, sweetest, nicest, kindest, and best.

Modals: *Must* expresses necessity. *Can* expresses ability and *can't* expresses inability.

PAIR PRACTICE   This exercise offers practice with *can.*

A: Can she swim like a fish?
B: Of course she can.
A: Can she sing like a bird?
B: Of course she can.
A: Can she bake a cake?
B: Of course she can.
A: Can she speak Chinese?
B: Of course she can.

PAIR PRACTICE

This exercise offers practice with the contractions *I'll* and *you'll.*

A: I'll help you, if you'll help me.
B: What do you want?
A: What do you have?
B: I'll help you, if you'll help me.

This exercise offers practice with the past tense irregular forms *saw, heard,* and *found.*

A: I was deep in the forest.
I saw something there.
B: Tell me, quickly.
What did you see?
A: I heard something there.
B: Tell me, quickly.
What did you hear?
A: I found something there.
B: Tell me, quickly.
What did you find?

RETELLING THE STORY

Write these sentences on the board or read them out loud. Ask your students to correct the statements.

1. The father in this story wasn't very proud of his daughter.

2. The daughter really knew how to spin straw into gold.

3. Rumpelstiltskin was a very big man.

4. He was dressed all in purple.

5. The King wanted to marry the girl because she cooked well.

6. Rumpelstiltskin tried to spin the straw into gold, but he couldn't do it.

7. The girl promised to marry Rumpelstiltskin if he turned all the straw into gold.

8. The Queen wasn't able to guess Rumpelstiltskin's name and had to give him her child.

THE FISHERMAN AND HIS WIFE

SUMMARY

Once upon a time, a fisherman and his wife lived in a house by the sea. The fisherman loved to go out alone in his boat, and sit and fish. One night while he was quietly fishing, he felt his fishing pole begin to shake, rattle, and roll. He began to pull in his line very slowly and carefully. After a moment, he saw the head of a very large fish.

"I wonder what kind of fish it is," said the fisherman. The fish answered, "I'm a flounder." The fisherman couldn't believe that he had caught a talking fish. The fish said that he was a magic fish and if the fisherman threw him back in the sea, he would give the fisherman anything he wanted.

The fisherman agreed to throw the flounder back in the sea, but couldn't think of anything to ask for. The fisherman soon went home and told his wife what happened. The wife got very upset when she found out her husband didn't ask for anything. She sent her husband back to the flounder and told him to ask for a house with nine rooms.

The flounder gave the fisherman and his wife the house and they were happy for awhile. Then one day, the wife had an idea. "I want you to be King," she said to her husband. The fisherman thought that was the worst idea he'd ever heard. "Then I'll be King. Go to the flounder. Tell him I want to be King," she said. So the fisherman went down to the sea and called the flounder. When the flounder came, the fisherman told the fish about his wife's wishes. "Go home, my friend. Your wife is King," said the flounder.

The fisherman and his wife, the King, lived together happily in a castle for awhile, but one morning the fisherman's wife had another idea. "Go to the flounder. Tell him I want to be Emperor," she said. And so the fisherman went back to the sea, and for the third time called the flounder. Just as before, the flounder appeared and granted the wife's wishes.

The fisherman and his wife, the Emperor, lived together happily for awhile, but one morning the fisherman's wife had another idea. "I want to make the stars shine. I want to make the sun rise," cried the wife. She told her husband to go to the flounder and ask for these things. And so once again, the fisherman went down to the sea, took a very deep breath, and sadly called the flounder.

The flounder appeared and the fisherman told him what his wife wanted. The flounder got very upset and swam down into the angry sea. When the flounder came back, he told the fisherman that the answer was no. The fisherman went home, and found that all the things the flounder had given them were gone. The fisherman didn't miss the big house or the time when his wife was King. He only missed the sound of the flounder's voice, but the fisherman never saw the flounder again.

STRUCTURE NOTES   This fairy tale offers practice with:

Plurals: Notice the /z/ sound of the plural *s* in fins, rooms, eyes, heads, tails, scales, things, and stars. Notice the /s/ sound of the plural in moments.

Possessive S: mermaid's tale and fisherman's wife.

Present Tense Third Person -S: brings, sounds, wants, does, and hates.

Present Continuous Tense: *I'm listening. The fisherman's wife is wearing a crown. What are you saying?* The present continuous tense describes an action that is currently taking place.

Past Continuous Tense: *Her eyes were shining. His wife was sitting inside wearing a crown.* The past continuous tense describes an action that was going on in the past.

Present Perfect Tense: *I've never seen such a thing in my life, when he had finished,* and *I've heard enough.* The present perfect tense is used to describe vague, indefinite past time.

Future, Will: *I will give you anything. It will be yours. Throw me back and you will see. What'll we do with four rooms? I'll be King.*

Imperative Statements: *Listen carefully. Tell me what you want. Tell him. Tell that flounder nine rooms. Go home. Call the flounder. Wake up. Go to the flounder. Speak up. Stop it.* Imperative statements are usually commands that do not have a stated subject but the implied subject *you.*

If-Clauses: *But if that's too hard for you to do . . . . If you won't, I will. If he won't, she will.*

Comparatives and Superlatives: strangest, bigger, worst, and better.

Modals: *Have to* and *must* express necessity or certainty. *Can't* expresses inability.

PAIR PRACTICE

This exercise offers practice with the vowel reduction of *and* to *'n.*

A: Sit and fish and wait for a bite.
B: Sit and fish and wait for a bite.
A: Sit and fish and wait for a bite from a fish
   at the bottom of the sea.

This exercise offers practice with the disappearing *h* sound in *keep him, take him, eat him, throw him,* and *pick him up* (*him* becomes *'im*).

A: Keep him, keep him.
   Take him home and eat him.
   Don't throw him back, no.
   Don't throw him back.
B: Pick him up and throw him back.
   Pick him up and throw him back.
   Throw him back.
   Throw him back.
A: Don't throw him back.
B: Throw him back.
   Throw him back.
A: Don't throw him back.

This exercise offers practice with the third person *s* (wants), plural *s* (rooms), possessive *s* (hers), and questions with *what, what kind of,* and *how many.*

A: What does she want?
B: She wants a house.
A: What kind of house?
B: A big house.
A: How many rooms?
B: Nine rooms.
A: The house is hers.
   Go home.

RETELLING THE STORY

Write these sentences on the board or read them out loud. Ask your students to correct the statements.

1. The fisherman was a very <u>impatient</u> man.

2. He fished all day long <u>but he didn't catch anything</u>.

3. He caught a nice big fish and <u>took it home to eat it</u>.

4. The fish was a <u>singing</u> fish.

5. The fisherman <u>wanted</u> to be King.

6. The fisherman's wife <u>didn't want anything at all</u>.

7. The flounder <u>didn't keep his promise</u> to the fisherman.

8. The flounder and the fisherman <u>stayed good friends for many years</u>.

Jazz Chant

FAIRY TALES

CAROLYN GRAHAM

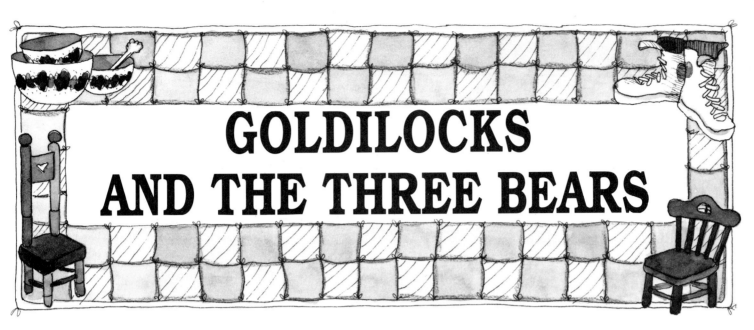

GOLDILOCKS AND THE THREE BEARS

NARRATOR
MAMA BEAR
PAPA BEAR
BABY BEAR
GOLDILOCKS
VOICE OF THE HOUSE
CHORUS

NARRATOR　　　Once upon a time there were three bears.

CHORUS　　　Three what?

NARRATOR　　　Three bears.
Once upon a time there were three bears.

CHORUS　　　How many bears?

NARRATOR　　　Three bears.
One *(clap)*.
Two *(clap clap)*.
Three bears.
One *(clap)*.
Two *(clap clap)*.
Three bears.
First there was the Mama, Mama Bear.

CHORUS	M A M A, Mama Bear.
NARRATOR	Then there was the Papa, Papa Bear.
CHORUS	P A P A, Papa Bear. Here comes Mama. Here comes Papa. Here they come. Mama and Papa. Mama loves Papa. Papa loves Mama. Mama and Papa love Baby Bear.
NARRATOR	Who loves Mama?
CHORUS	Papa loves Mama.
NARRATOR	Who loves Papa?
CHORUS	Mama loves Papa. Mama loves Papa. Papa loves Mama. Mama and Papa love Baby Bear.
MAMA BEAR	Where's Baby Bear? Where's Baby Bear?
CHORUS	Baby Bear, Baby Bear. Where's Baby Bear? We want Baby Bear, Baby Bear, Baby Bear! Where's Baby Bear, Baby Bear, Baby Bear?
PAPA BEAR	Look, look. Look over there. Look over there. It's Baby Bear.

BABY BEAR	B for Baby.
	B for Baby Bear.
	B for Baby.
	B for Baby Bear.
	B for Baby.
	B for Baby Bear.
	B stands for Baby.
	B stands for Bear.
	B B stands for Baby Bear.
	B stands for Baby.
	B stands for Bear.
	B B stands for Baby Bear.
NARRATOR	Once upon a time there were three bears.

CHORUS   One *(clap)*.
Two *(clap clap)*.
Three bears.

NARRATOR   One morning the three bears were busy getting ready for breakfast.

PAPA BEAR   I'll make the porridge.

MAMA BEAR   I'll pour the milk.

BABY BEAR   I'll set the table.
I'll set the table.

CHORUS   And they did *(clap clap)*.
And they did *(clap clap)*.
Baby set the table.
Mama poured the milk.
Papa made the porridge,
and they all sat down.

NARRATOR   Who set the table?

CHORUS   Baby set the table.

NARRATOR   Who poured the milk?

CHORUS   Mama poured the milk.

NARRATOR   Who made the porridge?

CHORUS   Papa made the porridge.
Papa made the porridge,
and they all sat down.
They all sat down.
They all sat down.
They all sat down, and started to eat.

BABY BEAR   Ow, wow! Hot, hot, hot!

4

MAMA BEAR	Ow, wow! Hot, hot, hot!
PAPA BEAR	Ow, wow! Hot, hot, hot!
NARRATOR	And they all jumped up, and danced around the table shouting, "Hot, hot, much too hot."
CHORUS	Hot, hot, much too hot. Hot, hot, much too hot. Much *(clap)* too *(clap)* hot *(clap clap)*. Much *(clap)* too *(clap)* hot *(clap clap)*.
PAPA BEAR	Let's go for a walk, and let it cool off.
MAMA BEAR	That's a good idea, let's go.

NARRATOR   And the three bears left, one by one, with their breakfast still on the table.

CHORUS   Glasses full of milk,
                 porridge in the bowls,
                 spoons in the porridge,
                 paper napkins.

                 Glasses full of milk,
                 porridge in the bowls,
                 spoons in the porridge,
                 paper napkins.

                 Spoons, glasses, bowls,
                 and napkins.
                 Spoons, glasses, bowls,
                 and napkins.

                 Glasses full of milk,
                 porridge in the bowls,
                 spoons in the porridge,
                 paper napkins.

NARRATOR   As soon as the bears left, the house felt empty and sad. There was no one there, not even a bear.

CHORUS   No one there, not even a bear.

**VOICE OF
THE HOUSE**   This is awful.
                 I feel bad.
                 I feel lonely.
                 I feel sad.
                 Empty table.
                 Empty chairs.
                 It's lonely here
                 without the bears.

6

NARRATOR Now the house felt so lonely for the bears, he began to sing a sad little song.

VOICE OF THE HOUSE (Melody: Skip to My Lou)

This is awful.
I feel bad.
I feel lonely.
I feel sad.
Empty table.
Empty chairs.
It's lonely here
without the bears.

NARRATOR Suddenly the house heard a noise.

VOICE OF THE HOUSE Oh, what's that?
What's that?
Who's there?
Oh, what's that?
I hope it's a bear.

CHORUS What's that?
Who's there?
What's that?
Who's there?
What's that?
Who's there?
I hope it's a bear.

NARRATOR	But it wasn't a bear. It was a little girl, a little girl with golden hair.
CHORUS	What's your name? What's your name?
GOLDILOCKS	Everybody calls me Goldilocks.
CHORUS	What did you say?
GOLDILOCKS	Goldilocks.
CHORUS	Goldilocks, Goldilocks. Say it again.
GOLDILOCKS	Goldilocks.
VOICE OF THE HOUSE	What a beautiful name!
NARRATOR	Goldilocks was surprised when she saw the bears' house.
GOLDILOCKS	What a surprise! What a beautiful house! I wonder if anybody's home.
NARRATOR	First she knocked on the door.
GOLDILOCKS	*Knock, knock.* Is anybody home? *Knock, knock.* Is anybody home?
NARRATOR	No one answered, so she knocked again.
GOLDILOCKS	*Knock, knock.* Is anybody home?
VOICE OF THE HOUSE	Come right in. Come in and sit down. The door's unlocked. Come in and sit down.

NARRATOR	She peeked through the window and knocked at the door. Nobody answered, so she knocked once more.
GOLDILOCKS	*Knock, knock.* Is anybody home? *Knock, knock.* Is anybody home?
VOICE OF THE HOUSE	Come right in. Come in and sit down. The door's unlocked. Come in and sit down.
NARRATOR	Goldilocks was afraid to enter an empty house alone. But the voice of the house sounded friendly, so she opened the door and walked in.

GOLDILOCKS   Look at the table,
set for three.
I hope there's a place
just right for me.

NARRATOR   First she sat down in Papa Bear's
chair, and tasted his bowl of porridge.

GOLDILOCKS   Oh, no. This is too hot,
and the chair is too big.
Much too big.

CHORUS   Too hot, too big!
Much too hot, much too big!

NARRATOR   Then she sat down in Mama Bear's
chair, and tasted her bowl of porridge.

GOLDILOCKS   Oh, no. This is too cold,
and the chair is too hard.
Much too hard.

CHORUS   Too cold, too hard!
Much too cold, much too hard!

NARRATOR   Then she sat down in Baby Bear's
chair, and tasted his bowl of porridge.

GOLDILOCKS   Mmmm, this is good.
Not too hot and not too cold.
Mmmm, this is good.
This is just right.

CHORUS   Just right, just right.

NARRATOR   So she sat right there in Baby Bear's
chair. She ate his porridge and
drank his milk. In fact, she was having
a wonderful time, when all
of a sudden, the chair fell apart,
and Goldilocks fell on the floor.

GOLDILOCKS   Oh, dear. What a shame.
Such a nice little chair.
Oh, dear. What a shame.
I think I'll take a nap.

NARRATOR   She walked into the bedroom, and
saw Papa Bear's bed.

GOLDILOCKS   This bed's too big.
Much too big.

CHORUS   Try another one.
Try another one.

NARRATOR   Then she saw Mama Bear's bed.

GOLDILOCKS   This bed's too hard.
                   Much too hard.

CHORUS   Try another one.
                   Try another one.

NARRATOR   Then she saw Baby Bear's nice
                   little bed, and it looked just right.

CHORUS   Just right, just right.
                   Not too big and not too hard.
                   Just right, just right.

NARRATOR	The bed was so comfortable that Goldilocks put her head on the pillow, pulled the covers up to her chin, and fell fast asleep. While Goldilocks was asleep, the three bears came home. They were just getting ready to sit down at the table when Papa Bear shouted:
PAPA BEAR	Hey, what's this? Someone's been sitting in my chair! Someone's been eating my porridge!
CHORUS	Eating his porridge. Sitting in his chair. We saw the girl with golden hair.
MAMA BEAR	Me oh my oh me, what's this? Someone's been sitting in my chair. Someone's been eating my porridge, too.
CHORUS	Eating her porridge. Sitting in her chair. We saw the girl with golden hair.
BABY BEAR	Mama, Mama! Papa, Papa! Somebody ate my porridge!
MAMA BEAR PAPA BEAR	Oh, no!
BABY BEAR	Look at my chair. Look at my chair. Somebody broke my chair!

MAMA BEAR **PAPA BEAR**	Oh, no! What a shame. I wonder who broke his chair.
CHORUS	We know the girl who broke his chair. We saw the girl with golden hair.
NARRATOR	Papa Bear got up from the table, and walked into the bedroom. Mama Bear and Baby Bear followed him.
PAPA BEAR	Oh, no! Oh, no! Someone's been sleeping in my bed.
MAMA BEAR	Oh, no! Oh, no! Someone's been sleeping in my bed, too.
NARRATOR	Then Baby Bear saw his bed with Goldilocks asleep under the covers. He began to shout:
BABY BEAR	Mama, Mama! Papa, Papa! Come quickly, come quickly. Someone's been sleeping in my bed. And here she is! And here she is!

14

PAPA BEAR	Look! It's a girl!
MAMA BEAR	Where?
PAPA BEAR	There!

NARRATOR	Goldilocks woke up and saw the three bears. She jumped out of bed, ran out the door, and no one ever saw her again.
PAPA BEAR	Well, that's that!

MAMA BEAR	Yes, that's that!
BABY BEAR	Wowie, that's that!
VOICE OF THE HOUSE	Goldilocks, gone! What a shame. Goldilocks, what a beautiful name!

LITTLE RED RIDING HOOD

NARRATOR
LITTLE RED RIDING HOOD
MOTHER
GRANNY
BIG BAD WOLF
HUNTER
CHORUS

NARRATOR   This is the story of a girl and a wolf.

CHORUS   Good girl.
Good little girl.
Bad wolf.
Big bad wolf.
Good little, good little,
good little girl.
Big (*clap*).
Bad (*clap*).
Wolf (*clap clap*).

NARRATOR   This is the story of a good little girl.

CHORUS   Good little, good little,
good little girl.

NARRATOR   This is the story of a good little girl,
who listened to her mother, most
of the time.

CHORUS   Good girl.
Good little girl.
She listened to her mother,
most of the time.

NARRATOR   This is the story of a girl and a wolf.
And they called her Little Red Riding Hood.

CHORUS   Little Red.
Little Red Riding Hood.
Little Red.
Little Red Riding Hood.
How did she ever
get a name like that?

NARRATOR   Like what?

CHORUS	Like Little Red Riding Hood. How did she ever get a name like that?
NARRATOR	She always wore a hood on her head, a little red riding hood. Her granny made it for her, and she wore it all the time. Little Red Riding Hood was a good little girl, most of the time.
CHORUS	Good girl. Good little girl. She listened to her mother, most of the time.
NARRATOR	When Mama said, "Go," she went (*clap clap*). When Mama said, "Stay," she stayed (*clap clap*). When Mama said, "Sit," she sat (*clap clap*). When Mama said, "Play," she played (*clap clap*).
CHORUS	When Mama said, "Go," she went (*clap clap*). When Mama said, "Stay," she stayed (*clap clap*). When Mama said, "Sit," she sat (*clap clap*). When Mama said, "Play," she played (*clap clap*).
NARRATOR	Little Red Riding Hood was a good little girl, most of the time.
CHORUS	Was she good?

NARRATOR Yes, she was.

CHORUS Was she very good?

NARRATOR Yes, she was.

CHORUS Did she listen to her mother?

NARRATOR Yes, she did.

CHORUS All of the time?

NARRATOR Most of the time. Little Red Riding Hood was a good little girl, most of the time. One morning Little Red Riding Hood was sleeping. She woke up when she heard her mother's voice.

MOTHER Wake up, wake up. It's time to get up.

LITTLE RED RIDING HOOD Mmmm, something smells like peanut butter. Something smells like chocolate. Chocolate peanut butter cookies. Chocolate peanut butter cookies.

MOTHER Please sit down. Eat your breakfast. These cookies are for Granny. She's home alone and sick in bed. Please visit her this morning.

CHORUS Poor Granny. What a shame. Home alone and sick in bed. Poor Granny. What a shame. Home alone and sick in bed.

LITTLE RED RIDING HOOD	Poor Granny. All alone. Of course, I'll go to see her.
MOTHER	Now Little Red Riding Hood, please sit down, and listen to me carefully.
LITTLE RED RIDING HOOD	`Yes, Mama. I'm listening.
MOTHER	Go straight to Granny's house.
LITTLE RED RIDING HOOD	Yes, Mama. I will.
MOTHER	Don't stop along the way.
LITTLE RED RIDING HOOD	No, Mama. I won't.
MOTHER	Don't talk to strangers.
LITTLE RED RIDING HOOD	No, Mama. I won't.
MOTHER	Be very careful.
LITTLE RED RIDING HOOD	Oh, Mama. I will.

NARRATOR   So Little Red Riding Hood kissed her mother good-bye. She took the basket of cookies, and walked along the path in the woods to Granny's house. She was skipping along happily when suddenly, a big wolf came out of the woods.

CHORUS   Watch out for the wolf.
Watch out. Watch out.
Watch out for the wolf.
Watch out!
The wolf is big.
The wolf is bad.
Watch out for the wolf.
Watch out!

NARRATOR	But Little Red Riding Hood forgot everything her mother said about not talking to strangers. When the wolf spoke to her, she spoke right back.
WOLF	Good morning, my dear. How are you this morning?
LITTLE RED RIDING HOOD	I'm fine, thank you. How are you?
WOLF	Just fine, my dear. What's your name?
CHORUS	Don't tell, don't tell. Mama told you not to tell. Mama told you not to tell, and not to talk to strangers.
LITTLE RED RIDING HOOD	My name is Little Red Riding Hood.
WOLF	I'm very happy to meet you. I've heard so many nice things about you.
LITTLE RED RIDING HOOD	You have?
WOLF	Oh, yes. Everyone says you're a good little girl.
LITTLE RED RIDING HOOD	They do? Thank you very much. You're very kind.
WOLF	What's that smell?
CHORUS	Don't tell, don't tell.

WOLF	What's that smell? What's that smell? Do I smell cookies?
LITTLE RED RIDING HOOD	Yes, you do. Chocolate peanut butter cookies. Mama made them for Granny. She's home alone and sick in bed. I'm on my way to see her.
CHORUS	Home alone and sick in bed. Mama told you not to tell.
WOLF	What a nice little girl. Where does Granny live? Is it far from here?
CHORUS	Don't tell, don't tell. Mama told you not to tell.
LITTLE RED RIDING HOOD	Granny lives in the little pink house. The little pink house at the end of this path.
WOLF	I know the house. I have an idea. Look over here. Look at the flowers. Why don't you pick some for Granny? Stop for awhile, stop for awhile. Pick some flowers for your Granny!
LITTLE RED RIDING HOOD	What a good idea!
CHORUS	Don't stop, don't stop. Mama told you not to stop.

Mama told you not to stop,
and not to talk to strangers.

NARRATOR

Little Red Riding Hood thought the
wolf's idea was just fine. She
stopped and picked the flowers
while the wolf ran as fast as he could
to Granny's house. He knocked
three times on the little front door.

Knock, knock, knock.

GRANNY

Yes? Who's there?

WOLF

(trying to sound like Little Red Riding Hood)
It's me, Little Red Riding Hood,
with a basket of cookies from Mama.

GRANNY

Come in, my dear, come in.
Come in and see your Granny.

NARRATOR	So the big bad wolf opened the door, found old Granny sick in bed, and gobbled her up in one big bite. Then he went to the closet and put on some of Granny's clothes. The big bad wolf climbed into bed to wait for Little Red Riding Hood. He pulled the covers up around his chin, and sat and waited and sat and waited.
WOLF	Where is that girl? What's the matter with her?
NARRATOR	He didn't have to wait very long. In a few moments he heard Little Red Riding Hood knock at the door.
LITTLE RED RIDING HOOD	Yoo hoo, Granny. It's me. It's me, Little Red Riding Hood.

WOLF	(pretending to be Granny) Come in, my dear, come in. Come in and see your Granny.
LITTLE RED RIDING HOOD	Where are you, Granny?
WOLF	I'm here in bed. Come in, my dear. Come in and let me see you.
CHORUS	Oh, no. Don't go. That's not Granny. Don't go.
NARRATOR	Little Red Riding Hood walked into the bedroom with her arms full of cookies and flowers. She stopped when she saw the wolf in bed.
WOLF	Come here, my dear.
CHORUS	Look at those ears.
WOLF	Here, near your Granny.
LITTLE RED RIDING HOOD	Oh, Granny. What big ears you have!
WOLF	The better to hear you with. Come here, my dear.
CHORUS	Look at those eyes.
WOLF	Here, near your Granny.
LITTLE RED RIDING HOOD	Oh, Granny. What big eyes you have!

WOLF	The better to see you with. Come here, my dear.
CHORUS	Look at those teeth.
WOLF	Here, near your Granny.
LITTLE RED RIDING HOOD	Oh, Granny. What big teeth you have.
WOLF	The better to eat you with.
NARRATOR	And just as he spoke, the wolf jumped up, and gobbled Little Red Riding Hood up in one big bite.
CHORUS	Oh, no! Oh, no! We told you so. We told you so.
NARRATOR	Now, the wolf was full. So he climbed back into Granny's bed and fell fast asleep. Then he began to snore. He snored louder and louder. A friendly hunter walking by the house heard the noise and stopped.
HUNTER	What's that sound? It's very loud. I'll stop and see if Granny's OK.
NARRATOR	The hunter knocked, but no one answered. He opened the door and went in. He heard someone snoring in Granny's bedroom. So he peeked into the bedroom, and saw the big bad wolf in Granny's bed.

HUNTER   Look at that wolf in Granny's bed.
I think he gobbled her up.

NARRATOR   The hunter cut a hole in the wolf's
stomach. To his great surprise, out
popped Little Red Riding Hood. The
wolf didn't even wake up. He just
thought he was having a very bad dream.

HUNTER   Good heavens. Who are you?

LITTLE RED   I'm Little Red Riding Hood.
RIDING HOOD

HUNTER   But where's your Granny?

GRANNY   Here I am.

NARRATOR   And out climbed Granny,
tired but happy.

GRANNY AND LITTLE RED RIDING HOOD	Oh, my. What a day!
LITTLE RED RIDING HOOD	Quick, quick! Let's put some stones inside the wolf. They will make him heavy so he can't get up.
HUNTER	Good idea!
GRANNY	Great idea!
NARRATOR	And they filled the wolf's stomach with heavy stones. He was dreaming a dream about girls and grannies and when he woke up, he had such a terrible stomachache, he fell right down and died.
LITTLE RED RIDING HOOD	Is he dead?
HUNTER	Oh, yes. Yes, he is. He's dead.
GRANNY	Are you sure?
HUNTER	Oh, yes. Yes, I am. He's dead. He's dead. He's dead. The wolf is dead! The big bad wolf is dead! Hooray!

CHORUS

He's dead. He's dead.
The wolf is dead!
The big bad wolf is dead!
Hooray!

NARRATOR

And this is the end of the story of
the girl, who listened to her mother,
most of the time.

CHORUS

Good girl.
Good little girl.
She listened to her mother,
most of the time.

CHICKEN LITTLE

NARRATOR
CHICKEN LITTLE
HENNY PENNY
COCKY LOCKY
DUCKY WUCKY
GOOSEY WOOSEY
TURKEY LURKEY
FOXY WOXY
CHORUS

NARRATOR One morning Chicken Little woke up early, and decided to go for a walk. The sun was shining. It was a beautiful day and as she was walking under the old oak tree, a small acorn fell, *plop,* and landed right on her head.

CHICKEN LITTLE Hey, what was that?
What was that? Oh, no!
The sky is falling in!

CHORUS Run chicken, run chicken.
Run Chicken Little Little.
Run, chicken, run.

The sky is falling in.
Chicken Little, run, run.
Chicken Little, run, run.
Run Chicken Little.
The sky is falling in.

CHICKEN LITTLE   I must tell the King.
I must tell the King.
A piece of the sky
fell on my head.
I must tell the King.

CHORUS   You must tell the King.
You must tell the King.
The sky is falling in.
You must tell the King.

NARRATOR   Chicken Little began to walk a
little faster down the road toward
the King's castle. On the way, she
met her old friend Henny Penny.

HENNY PENNY   Good morning, Chicken Little.
Where are you going?
What's your hurry?
Chicken Little, what's your hurry?
Can't you say hello?

CHICKEN LITTLE   I can't stop now.
I'm going to see the King.
The sky is falling in.
I must tell the King.

HENNY PENNY   What did you say?
What did you say?

CHICKEN LITTLE   The sky is falling in.

HENNY PENNY   That's what I thought you said.

CHORUS   Run, chick, run.
The sky is falling in.
Run, chick, run.
You must tell the King.

HENNY PENNY   Tell me again. What fell?

CHICKEN LITTLE   A piece of the sky.

HENNY PENNY   When did it fall?

CHICKEN LITTLE   Just a minute ago.

HENNY PENNY   A minute ago? Oh, no!
We must tell the King.

CHORUS   You must tell the King.
You must tell the King.
The sky is falling in.
You must tell the King.

NARRATOR   So Chicken Little and Henny Penny
hurried together down the road
toward the King's castle. On the way,
they met their old friend Cocky Locky.

COCKY LOCKY

Hello, Chicken Little.
Hello, Henny Penny.
Where are you going?
What's your hurry?
Slow down, Henny Penny.
What's your hurry, Chicken Little?

CHORUS

Slow down, slow down.
What's your hurry, Chicken Little?
Slow down, slow down.
What's your hurry, Henny Penny?
Slow down, slow down.

HENNY PENNY

We can't slow down.
We can't slow down.
We must tell the King.

CHORUS   Tell the King. Tell the King.
                    They must tell the King.
                    They can't slow down.
                    They must tell the King.

COCKY LOCKY   Tell the King what?
                    What's the matter? What's wrong?
                    What are you going to tell the King?

CHORUS   What's the matter? What's wrong?
                    What's the matter? What's wrong?
                    What's wrong? What's wrong?
                    What's the matter? What's wrong?

HENNY PENNY

The sky is falling in.
The sky is falling in.

CHORUS

Run, chick, run.
The sky is falling in.
Tell the King. Tell the King.
The sky is falling in.
Cocky Locky, Henny Penny,
Chicken Little, run!
The sky is falling in.
The sky is falling in.

COCKY LOCKY

Who said that?
Who said that?
Henny Penny, how do you know?

HENNY PENNY

Chicken Little told me so.

COCKY LOCKY

Chicken Little, how do you know?

CHICKEN LITTLE

How do I know?
A piece of the sky
fell on my head.
Just a minute ago.

COCKY LOCKY

Oh, no. What'll we do?
Oh, my. What'll we do?
The sky is falling in.
We must tell the King.

NARRATOR

And so Cocky Locky joined Chicken Little and Henny Penny. The three of them hurried together down the road toward the King's castle. On the way, they met their old friend Ducky Wucky.

37

DUCKY WUCKY   Chicken Little, Henny Penny,
Cocky Locky, HI!
Where are you going?
Where are you going?
Chicken Little, Henny Penny,
Cocky Locky, HEY!
Can I come, too? Can I come, too?

CHORUS   Chicken Little, Henny Penny,
Cocky Locky, HI!
Chicken Little, Henny Penny,
Cocky Locky, HEY!
Chicken Little, Henny Penny,
Cocky Locky, HO!
Can I come, too? Can I come, too?

COCKY LOCKY   We're going to see the King.
We have to see the King.

DUCKY WUCKY   Why do you have to see the King?

COCKY LOCKY   The sky is falling in!

DUCKY WUCKY   The sky? Oh, my.
The sky is falling in?

COCKY LOCKY   That's right, that's right.
The sky is falling in.

38

DUCKY WUCKY	Cocky Locky, how do you know?
COCKY LOCKY	Henny Penny told me so.
DUCKY WUCKY	Henny Penny, how do you know?
HENNY PENNY	Chicken Little told me so.
DUCKY WUCKY	Chicken Little, how do you know?
CHICKEN LITTLE	How do I know? A piece of the sky fell on my head. Just a minute ago.
DUCKY WUCKY	Oh, no. What'll we do? Oh, my. What'll we do? The sky is falling in. We must tell the King.
NARRATOR	And so Ducky Wucky joined Chicken Little and Henny Penny and Cocky Locky. The four of them hurried together down the road toward the King's castle. On the way, they met their old friend Goosey Woosey.

GOOSEY WOOSEY	Chicken Little, Henny Penny. Cocky Locky, Ducky Wucky. Where are you going? What's your hurry? Can't you say hello?
DUCKY WUCKY	We can't slow down. We can't slow down. We don't have time to say hello. We must see the King.
GOOSEY WOOSEY	Why do you want to do that? Why do you want to do that? You know the King has more important things to do than talk to you. Why do you want to do that? Why do you want to do that?
CHORUS	The King! The King! Everyone wants to see the King! The King has more important things to do than talk to you. Talk to you, talk to you. Nobody wants to talk to you. The King has more important things to do than talk to you.
DUCKY WUCKY	We have to see the King. The sky is falling in.
GOOSEY WOOSEY	The sky is falling in? Ducky Wucky, how do you know?
DUCKY WUCKY	Cocky Locky told me so.
GOOSEY WOOSEY	Cocky Locky, how do you know?

40

COCKY LOCKY	Henny Penny told me so.
GOOSEY WOOSEY	Henny Penny, how do you know?
HENNY PENNY	Chicken Little told me so.
GOOSEY WOOSEY	Chicken Little, how do you know?
CHICKEN LITTLE	How do I know? A piece of the sky fell on my head. Just a minute ago. We must tell the King.
NARRATOR	So Goosey Woosey joined Chicken Little and Henny Penny and Cocky Locky and Ducky Wucky. The five of them hurried together down the road toward the King's castle. On the way, they met their old friend Turkey Lurkey.

TURKEY LURKEY　　Where are you going?
　　　　　　　　　　　What's your hurry?
　　　　　　　　　　　Slow down, slow down.

GOOSEY WOOSEY　　We can't stop now.
　　　　　　　　　　　We must see the King.

TURKEY LURKEY　　Why do you have to see the King?

GOOSEY WOOSEY　　The sky is falling in.
　　　　　　　　　　　Someone has to tell the King.
　　　　　　　　　　　The sky is falling in.

TURKEY LURKEY　　The sky is falling in?
　　　　　　　　　　　How do you know?

GOOSEY WOOSEY　　Chicken Little told Henny Penny,
　　　　　　　　　　　then Henny Penny told Cocky Locky,
　　　　　　　　　　　Cocky Locky told Ducky Wucky,
　　　　　　　　　　　and Ducky Wucky told me.

TURKEY LURKEY　　Is that true? Then I'll come, too.
　　　　　　　　　　　We must tell the King.
　　　　　　　　　　　The sky is falling in.
　　　　　　　　　　　We must tell the King.

42

NARRATOR   And down the road they went, just as fast as they could go. Chicken Little and Henny Penny, Cocky Locky and Ducky Wucky, Goosey Woosey and Turkey Lurkey hurried together toward the King's castle. On the way, they met Foxy Woxy.

CHORUS   Watch out for the fox.
He'll eat you up.
Watch out for the fox. Watch out!
He'll eat you up.
He'll eat you up.
Watch out for the fox. Watch out!

NARRATOR   Foxy Woxy saw Chicken Little and her friends hurrying down the road. He smiled a foxy smile and said to himself:

FOXY WOXY   Ah ha!
What's this coming down the road?
It looks like a tasty Sunday dinner.
Mmmm, mmmm, I can't wait.
Mmmm, mmmm, I can't wait.

NARRATOR	Then he turned to Chicken Little, and in his most polite and friendly voice said:
FOXY WOXY	Good morning, my dear. Where are you going? Where are you going this morning?
CHICKEN LITTLE	Oh, Mr. Fox, haven't you heard? The sky is falling in. We must tell the King. We must tell the King.
NARRATOR	Now, Foxy Woxy was a clever fellow. He didn't believe for a minute that the sky was really falling in. He took a long look at the sky, and then turned to Chicken Little and said:
FOXY WOXY	Hey, you're right. Here it comes! The sky is falling in. Follow me. I know the way. I'll take you to the King.
NARRATOR	So Chicken Little and Henny Penny, Cocky Locky and Ducky Wucky, Goosey Woosey and Turkey Lurkey all followed Foxy Woxy, and no one ever saw them again. And nobody told the King.

44

THE THREE BILLY GOATS GRUFF

NARRATOR
BIG BILL
WILL
LITTLE BILLY
THE TROLL
CHORUS

NARRATOR

This is the story
of the Billy Goats Gruff.

CHORUS

Three Billy Goats.
Billy Goats Gruff.
One (*clap*).
Two (*clap clap*).
Three Billy Goats.
Three Billy Goats.
Billy Goats Gruff.

NARRATOR

Now, the oldest Billy Goat Gruff was Bill.

CHORUS

Big Bill.
Billy Goat Gruff.
Rough and tough.
Billy Goat Gruff.
Rough and tough.
Billy Goat Gruff.

BIG BILL   Rough and tough,
and ready to go.
I'm a Billy Goat Gruff
from head to toe.

CHORUS   Rough and tough,
and ready to go.
He's a Billy Goat Gruff
from head to toe.

NARRATOR   Big Bill's brother was a goat named Will.

CHORUS	Bill's brother. Big Bill's brother. Big Bill's brother was a goat named Will.
WILL	My name is Will. I'm a Billy Goat Gruff. My brother Bill is very tough. I'm not as big or smart as Bill. I'm just a goat. You can call me Will.
NARRATOR	Bill and Will had a little baby brother. They called him Little Billy.
LITTLE BILLY	They call me Little Billy Goat Gruff. I'm not very big. I'm not very tough. I'm not very old. I'm not very rough. But, hey! I'm a Billy Goat Gruff.
CHORUS	Hey! He's a Billy Goat Gruff.
BIG BILL **WILL** **LITTLE BILLY**	We're the rough, tough Billy Goats Gruff. Rough and tough. Billy Goats Gruff.
NARRATOR	One day the three Billy Goats Gruff decided to visit their favorite hill, and look for something to eat.
LITTLE BILLY	I'm going to look for butterflies. I'm going to look for daisies.
WILL	I'm going to look for green grass. Fresh, sweet green grass. I'm going to look for green grass. He's going to look for daisies.

CHORUS	Fresh, sweet green grass. Will's going to look for green grass. Billy's going to look for butterflies. Billy's going to look for daisies.
NARRATOR	Big Bill didn't care what he ate as long as there was plenty of it.
BIG BILL	I'll eat anything, anything at all. Tin cans, pancakes. Carrot tops, milk shakes. I'll eat anything, anything at all. Peanut butter, butterflies. Ice cream, golf balls. I'll eat anything, anything at all. Dandelions, daisies. Green grass, green cheese. I'll eat anything, anything at all.
CHORUS	Tin cans?
BIG BILL	Anything.
CHORUS	Pancakes?
BIG BILL	Anything.
CHORUS	Carrot tops?
BIG BILL	Anything, anything at all.
CHORUS	Milk shakes?
BIG BILL	Anything.

CHORUS	Peanut butter?
BIG BILL	Anything.
CHORUS	Butterflies?
BIG BILL	Anything, anything at all.
CHORUS	Ice cream, golf balls?
BIG BILL	Anything, anything.
CHORUS	Dandelions, daisies?
BIG BILL	Anything, anything.
CHORUS	Green grass, green cheese?

BIG BILL

I'll eat anything.
I'll eat anything,
anything at all.

NARRATOR

And so the three Billy Goats Gruff
began to walk to their favorite hill.
On their way, they had to cross a
bridge over a river. But a terrible
troll lived under the bridge.

CHORUS

BAAA! BAAA!
Watch out for the troll!
Watch out! Watch out!
He'll eat you up,
if you don't watch out.
Watch out for the troll!
Watch out! Watch out!
Watch out for the troll, watch out!
The troll eats goats, watch out.
He'll eat you up,
if you don't watch out.
Watch out for the troll, watch out!

NARRATOR	Little Billy got to the bridge first. He heard the lambs telling him to watch out for the troll, but he wasn't afraid. He was thinking of the butterflies and daisies on the hill. He hopped and skipped onto the bridge. His tiny little feet went pit pat, pit pat, pitter patter, pit pat.
CHORUS	Pitter patter Pit pat Pitter patter Pit pat Pitter pitter patter patter Pitter pat pat
NARRATOR	Suddenly, Little Billy heard the angry voice of the terrible troll.
TROLL	Who's there? What's that? What's that pit pat? Who's pitty pitty patting over my bridge?
CHORUS	Watch out, Little Billy! He'll eat you up! Watch out, Little Billy! Watch out!
LITTLE BILLY	Watch out for what?
CHORUS	For the troll!
LITTLE BILLY	For the what?
CHORUS	The troll, the troll.
LITTLE BILLY	The troll? What's a troll?

TROLL
I'll show him what a troll is!
EEEEEE OWWWWW
WUUUUU WOOOOO
I like to fight and bite!
I like to kick and slap!
I like to pinch and punch!
I like to push and shove!
I like to knock it down,
and drag it around,
then do it all over again.

LITTLE BILLY
WOW!

CHORUS
He likes to fight and bite!
He likes to kick and slap!
He likes to pinch and punch!
He likes to push and shove!
He likes to knock it down,
and drag it around,
then do it all over again.

TROLL
That's right!
Hey, little goat, what's your name?

LITTLE BILLY
Everybody calls me Billy.

TROLL
Billy? What a silly name.
I'll eat you up!
Silly Billy, silly Billy.

LITTLE BILLY
Please Mr. Troll, don't eat me.
I'm not fat, as you can see.
If you really want a thrill,
you ought to meet my brother, Will.

TROLL
Your brother Will?
Is he bigger than you?

LITTLE BILLY	Much bigger and fatter, too.
TROLL	Well, all right. I'll let you go.
NARRATOR	So Little Billy hurried off the bridge. Soon his brother Will came. Will wasn't really big or fat, but he was bigger and fatter than Little Billy. He made a lot of noise as he walked on the bridge.
CHORUS	Rat-a-tat-tat. Root-a-toot-toot. Rat-a-tat-rat-a-tat. Root-a-toot-toot.
TROLL	Hey, who's there? Who's there? What's that? What's that rat-a-tat, tat-tat-tat? It sounds like a nice big Billy Goat Gruff. I hope he's big enough to eat. Hey, who's there? Who's there? What's that? Stop that rat-a-tat, tat-tat-tat.

WILL	I'm Brother Will on my way to the hill.
CHORUS	Be careful Will, watch out, watch out! The troll will eat you up. That troll eats goats, watch out!
WILL	A troll? Where?
CHORUS	There!
WILL	Where?
TROLL	Right here, I'm right here. I've got you where I want you now. I think I'll eat you up!
WILL	Eat me up? Oh, no! Not that! Not me, not now, not here, not that! You must be confused. My name is Will. The one you want is brother Bill.

TROLL	Another brother? Another goat? How many brothers are there?
WILL	There are three of us, but two are small. Big fat Bill is the best of all.
TROLL	Big? Fat? Did you say fat?
WILL	That's what I said. Fat as a pig.
TROLL	What? A goat as fat as a pig?
WILL	That's right, you'll see. Don't look at me. You'll see how big a goat can be!
NARRATOR	And so Will hurried across just as his brother Bill came marching onto the bridge.
CHORUS	Clump, clump, clump. Bumpety, bump, bump. Here comes Bill. Clump, clump, clump. Here comes Bill. Bumpety, bump, bump.
TROLL	Hey, who's there? Who's there? What's that? Stop that clump, clump, bumpety, bump, bump. Who's that clumpety clumping over my bridge?
BIG BILL	Your bridge? Who are you?

TROLL	I'm the troll. I like to fight and bite. I like to kick and slap. I like to pinch and punch. I like to push and shove. I like to . . .
BIG BILL	(interrupting the troll) You're tall for a troll.
TROLL	What?
BIG BILL	I said you're tall for a troll. I thought trolls were small.
TROLL	Some trolls are small, some are tall. I am tall.
CHORUS	Some are tall. Some are small. Some aren't really trolls at all!
BIG BILL	A tall troll?
TROLL	That's right. You're smart for a goat.
BIG BILL	What you did say?
TROLL	I said you're smart for a goat. I thought goats were stupid.
BIG BILL	Some are stupid. Some are smart. Why don't you climb up here on the bridge? We'll see who's smarter, trolls or goats.

TROLL Goats are stupid. Trolls are smart.
Smarter than goats,
smarter than goats.

NARRATOR The troll climbed up onto the
bridge with Big Bill, and looked
him right in the eye.

TROLL Goats are stupid.
Trolls are smart.
Trolls are smarter than goats.
So there!

BIG BILL Come a little closer
to the edge of the bridge.
I can't hear you.
I can't hear you.

NARRATOR   The troll stepped closer and closer to the edge, and repeated his words in a loud voice.

TROLL   Trolls are smarter than goats.

BIG BILL   What?

TROLL   Trolls are smarter than goats.

NARRATOR   But just as he said the word "goats," Big Bill gave him a great big shove. The troll fell into the deep dark water. He sank like a stone to the bottom of the river, and no one ever saw him again.

CHORUS   Down down down down down to the bottom. He sank like a stone, down to the bottom, down to the bottom, and no one ever saw him again.

NARRATOR   And that was the end of the terrible troll, and the story of the Billy Goats Gruff.

THE THREE LITTLE PIGS

NARRATOR
BABY PIG
BROTHER
BIG BROTHER
MOTHER PIG
STRAW SELLER
BRICK SELLER
WOLF
CHORUS

NARRATOR   This is the story of the three little pigs.

CHORUS   One (*clap*).
Two (*clap*).
Three little pigs.

NARRATOR   The three little pigs all lived together
with their father and their mother.

CHORUS   One (*clap*). Two (*clap*).
Three little pigs.
All together, all together, all together
with their father and their mother.
One little. Two little. Three little pigs.
One (*clap*). Two (*clap*).
Three little pigs.

NARRATOR	One morning Mother Pig called her three sons and said:
MOTHER PIG	Boys?
THREE PIGS	Yes, Mother.
MOTHER PIG	Listen to me. Listen to what I have to say.
THREE PIGS	Yes, Mother dear. We're listening.
MOTHER PIG	You know that your father and I love you very much.
THREE PIGS	Yes, Mother dear. We know that.
MOTHER PIG	But now it is time for you to leave home, and go out into the world alone.
CHORUS	Leave home, leave home. Go out alone and leave home. Leave home, leave home. Go into the world alone.
MOTHER PIG	You're not babies anymore.
THREE PIGS	That's right, Mother dear.
MOTHER PIG	I have taught you everything I know. I hope you are ready for the world.
THREE PIGS	We are, Mama dear, we are.

MOTHER PIG	And I hope that the world is ready for you! Remember what I said about the wolf.
BABY PIG	The what?
MOTHER PIG	Remember what I said about the wolf.
BROTHER PIG BIG BROTHER PIG	We will.
MOTHER PIG	Never let a wolf in your door.
THREE PIGS	We won't.

CHORUS   Never let a wolf in your door.
Listen to your mama.
Listen to your mama.
Never let a wolf in your door.
Oh, no. Never let a wolf in your door.

MOTHER PIG   Good-bye, good-bye,
my darling sons.

THREE PIGS   Don't cry, Mother dear, good-bye.

MOTHER PIG   Remember my words.
Watch out for the wolf.
Never let a wolf in your door.

NARRATOR   And so the three little pigs left
home. They walked down the road
and Big Brother Pig told his
brothers to be careful of the wolf.
Soon the road split into three
directions. Big Brother Pig stopped
and said:

BIG BROTHER PIG   Now, we must each
choose our own road.
Remember what Mama said.
Watch out for the wolf.

BABY PIG	What'll I do if he comes to my door?
BIG BROTHER PIG	If he comes to your door, don't let him in, not by the hair of your chinny chin chin. And now good-bye. I'll take the road on the left.
BROTHER PIG	And I'll take the road on the right. Bye-bye.
BABY PIG	Which road do I take?
BIG BROTHER PIG	You'll take the one in the middle, little brother. Sweet little brother.
CHORUS	Sweet little brother.
THREE PIGS	Bye-bye, good luck. Bye-bye, dear brothers. So long, good luck, bye-bye.
NARRATOR	And the three little pigs each walked down a different road into the big world alone. Baby Pig was skipping down the road happily when he met a man carrying straw.

STRAW SELLER	Straw for sale. Straw for sale. Clean, fresh straw for sale.
BABY PIG	Good morning, sir. May I buy some straw? I need some straw to build a house, to keep the wolf away.
STRAW SELLER	A house of straw? A straw house?
BABY PIG	Yes, a house of straw, soft and warm, soft and warm, to keep the wolf away.
CHORUS	A house of straw, soft and warm, to keep the wolf away.
NARRATOR	Baby Pig bought three bundles of straw, and began to build his house. He finished it as fast as he could. It wasn't very pretty and it wasn't very good. But, it was his house and he loved it. When everything was ready, he stood back and looked at it for a long time. Then he went inside, locked the front door, lay down on the floor, and went to sleep. Suddenly there was a loud knock. *Knock, knock, knock.*
BABY PIG	Oh, my! What's that? Who's there?
WOLF	A friend.

BABY PIG	A friend? Whose friend? What friend?
CHORUS	Don't let him in. Don't let him in. Not by the hair of your chinny chin chin.
BABY PIG	Oh, no! It must be the wolf!
WOLF	Open the door! Let me in!
BABY PIG	Not by the hair of my chinny chin chin.
WOLF	Open the door! Let me in!
BABY PIG	Not by the hair of my chinny chin chin.

WOLF	Then I'll huff and I'll puff, and I'll blow your house down.
NARRATOR	And he huffed and puffed, and he blew the house down, and ate Baby Pig up in one big bite.
WOLF	Mmmm, mmmm! That was good!
NARRATOR	While all of this was happening, Baby Pig's brother was walking down the road. He too, met the man selling straw.
STRAW SELLER	Straw for sale. Straw for sale. Clean, fresh straw for sale.
CHORUS	Straw for sale. Straw for sale. Clean, fresh straw for sale.
BROTHER PIG	Oh, no! That's not for me! I want something stronger than straw. I'm going to build a house!
CHORUS	Stronger than straw. Stronger than straw. He wants something stronger than straw. Stronger than straw. Stronger than straw. He's going to build a house!
NARRATOR	And so Brother Pig continued down the road. Soon he met a man selling sticks.

STICK SELLER

Sticks for sale.
Sticks for sale.
Good, hard sticks for sale.
Good sticks, hard sticks.
Good, hard sticks for sale.

BROTHER PIG

Sticks are stronger than straw, yes.
Sticks are stronger than straw.
I'm going to build my house of sticks.
Sticks are stronger than straw.

CHORUS

Stronger than straw,
stronger than straw.
Sticks are stronger than straw.
He's going to build
his house of sticks.
Sticks are stronger than straw.

NARRATOR

Brother Pig bought the sticks, and
began to build his house. He worked
very hard all day. When it was
finished, he went inside, locked the
door, lay down on the floor, and
fell asleep. Suddenly there was a
loud knock.

Knock, knock, knock.

BROTHER PIG   Oh, my! What's that?

WOLF   Your brother.

BROTHER PIG   That's not my brother's voice.
Who's there?

WOLF   Open the door! Let me in!

CHORUS   Don't let him in.
Don't let him in.
Not by the hair
of your chinny chin chin.

BROTHER PIG   Oh, no! It must be the wolf!

WOLF   Open the door! Let me in!

BROTHER PIG   Not by the hair of my
chinny chin chin.

WOLF   Open the door! Let me in!

BROTHER PIG   Not by the hair of my
chinny chin chin.

WOLF   Then I'll huff and I'll puff,
and I'll blow your house down.

NARRATOR	The wolf huffed and he puffed, and he blew the house down. Then he ate Brother Pig up in one big bite.
WOLF	Mmmm, mmmm! That was good!
NARRATOR	While all of this was happening, Big Brother Pig was walking down the road. He too, met the man selling straw.
STRAW SELLER	Straw for sale. Straw for sale. Clean, fresh straw.
BIG BROTHER PIG	Oh, no! That's not for me. I want something stronger than straw. Much stronger than straw.
CHORUS	Stronger than straw. Stronger than straw. Much stronger than straw.
NARRATOR	Soon he met the man selling sticks.
STICK SELLER	Sticks for sale. Sticks for sale. Good, hard sticks.
BIG BROTHER PIG	Oh, no! That's not for me. I want something stronger than sticks. Stronger than sticks. Stronger than straw. Much stronger than sticks and straw.

NARRATOR	And so Big Brother Pig continued down the road. Soon he met a man selling bricks.
BRICK SELLER	Bricks for sale. Bricks for sale. Good, strong bricks.
BIG BROTHER PIG	That's what I want. Strong bricks. I'm going to build my house of bricks. Stronger than straw. Stronger than sticks. I want a house of bricks.
CHORUS	Sticks and straw. Sticks and straw. Sticks and straw and bricks. Bricks are stronger than sticks and straw. Bricks are stronger than sticks.
NARRATOR	Slowly and carefully, one by one, the pig built a house of bricks.
CHORUS	Slowly and carefully. One by one. Slowly and carefully. One by one.
NARRATOR	When he was finished, he went inside, locked the door, started a big fire in the fireplace, and hung a large cooking pot over the fire to make his dinner. The water in the pot was boiling when suddenly he heard a loud knock on the door.

Knock, knock, knock.

BIG BROTHER PIG   Oh, my! What's that?

WOLF   Open the door.
Open the door,
and you'll see who I am.

BIG BROTHER PIG   I know who you are.
I know, I know.

WOLF   Open the door! Let me in!

BIG BROTHER PIG   Not by the hair of my
chinny chin chin.

WOLF   Open the door! Let me in!

BIG BROTHER PIG   Not by the hair of my
chinny chin chin.

WOLF   Then I'll huff and I'll puff,
and I'll blow your house down.

BIG BROTHER PIG   Go ahead, go ahead.
Try it.

NARRATOR   The wolf huffed and he puffed, but
the house was so strong that he
couldn't blow it down no matter
how hard he tried. He was getting
very angry.

WOLF   Open the door, open the door!
Open the door right now!
If you don't open the door right now,
I'm coming down the chimney!

BIG BROTHER PIG   Good idea! Come right in!

NARRATOR   So the wolf jumped down the
chimney and fell right into the big
pot of boiling water. And that was
the end of the big bad wolf, and the
story of the three little pigs.

LITTLE RED HEN

NARRATOR
LITTLE RED HEN
DOG
CAT
DUCK
BABY CHICK CHORUS
CHICKEN CHORUS
ROOSTER CHORUS

CHICKEN CHORUS   Chickens in the yard working hard.
Chickens in the yard working hard.
Chickens in the yard
going cluck, cluck, cluck, cluck.

ROOSTER CHORUS   Roosters in the yard working hard.
Roosters in the yard working hard.
Roosters in the yard
going cock-a-doodle-do.

CHICKEN CHORUS   Chickens in the yard
going cluck, cluck, cluck, cluck.

BABY CHICK   Chicks in the yard working hard.
CHORUS   Chicks in the yard working hard.
Chicks in the yard
going peep, peep, peep, peep.

CHORUS (ALL)   Cluck cluck, peep peep,
cock-a-doodle-do.
Cluck cluck, peep peep,
cock-a-doodle-do.
Chickens in the yard working hard.
Chickens in the yard working hard.

NARRATOR   Once upon a time there was a Little
Red Hen who worked very hard from
nine to ten. She started every
morning at nine o'clock and worked
every evening till ten.

CHORUS (ALL)   Little Red Hen.
Little Red Hen.
She worked very hard
from nine to ten.
Going scratch, scratch,
scratch, scratch.
Pick it up, pick it up.
Scratch, scratch,
scratch, scratch.
Pick it up, pick it up.
Day and night
from nine to ten,
she worked very hard,
the Little Red Hen.

NARRATOR

There was a dog in the yard
with the Little Red Hen.
A lazy dog who went "bow wow wow."
There was a cat in the yard
with the Little Red Hen.
A crazy cat who went
"meow, meow, meow."

CHORUS (ALL)

Lazy dog, crazy cat,
there in the yard
with the Little Red Hen.

NARRATOR

There was a duck in the yard
with the Little Red Hen.
A duck who went "quack."
Quack, quack, quack, quack.

CHORUS (ALL)

Lazy dog, crazy cat,
and a duck who went "quack."
Quack, quack, quack, quack.

NARRATOR

Now the dog and the cat and the
duck who went "quack" loved to sit
around the yard, and watch the
Little Hen work. One day while
she was busy scratching in the yard,
she found some grains of wheat.

LITTLE RED HEN

Look! Look what I found!

DOG	What?
LITTLE RED HEN	Wheat. Some grains of wheat.
CAT (to DOG)	What? What did she find?
DOG	Wheat.
DUCK	What?
DOG	Wheat. Some grains of wheat.
CAT	Where?
DOG	There, there on the ground. She found some grains of wheat.
DUCK	Who cares what she found on the ground.
CAT	Not me.
CHORUS (ALL)	Who cares what she found on the ground. Scratch, scratch. Pick it up. Scratch, scratch. Pick it up. Who cares what she found on the ground!
DOG	What'll you do with the wheat?
CAT	What'll you do?
DUCK	What'll you do?
LITTLE RED HEN	Plant it, of course. Will you help?

DOG	I'm sorry, I can't.
LITTLE RED HEN (to CAT)	Will you?
CAT	Not me.
LITTLE RED HEN (to DUCK)	Will you?
DUCK	Oh, quack. Not me. I'm afraid I can't. I wish I could, but I'm afraid I can't.
LITTLE RED HEN	Then I'll have to do it myself.
NARRATOR	And she did. She planted the wheat all by herself. It grew and it grew, tall and strong.
LITTLE RED HEN	Today the wheat is ready to cut. Today's the day, today's the day.

CHORUS (ALL)	Today's the day to cut the wheat. Today's the day, today's the day.
LITTLE RED HEN	Who will help me cut the wheat?
DOG	I'm sorry, I can't.
LITTLE RED HEN (to CAT)	Will you?
CAT	Not me.
LITTLE RED HEN (to DUCK)	Will you?
DUCK	Oh, quack. Not me. I'm afraid I can't. I wish I could, but I'm afraid I can't.
CHORUS (ALL)	I wish I could, but I'm afraid I can't. I wish I could, but I'm afraid I can't.
LITTLE RED HEN	Then I'll have to do it myself.
NARRATOR	And she did. She cut the wheat all by herself, and when the job was finished, she said:
LITTLE RED HEN	Now who will take this wheat to the mill?
DOG	I'm sorry, I can't.
LITTLE RED HEN (to CAT)	Will you?

CAT   Not me.

LITTLE RED HEN   Will you?
(to DUCK)

DUCK   Oh, quack. Not me.
I'm afraid I can't.
I wish I could,
but I'm afraid I can't.

LITTLE RED HEN   Then I'll have to do it myself.
I found it.
I planted it.
I cut it.
Now I can take it to the mill myself.

CHORUS (ALL)   Oh, yes, I guess
she can take it to the mill.
Oh, yes, I guess she can.

NARRATOR	And she did. The Little Red Hen picked up the wheat, and carried it to the mill where it was ground into flour. Then she came back to the yard.
LITTLE RED HEN	Now who will help me bake the bread?
DOG	Bake the bread? I'm sorry, I can't.
LITTLE RED HEN	Who will help me bake the bread?
DOG	Not me.
CAT	Not me.
DUCK	Not me.
LITTLE RED HEN	I see. Oh, well. I'll have to do it myself.
NARRATOR	And so she baked the bread, and it was wonderful. When the bread was ready, the dog and the cat and the duck gathered around the Little Red Hen, waiting and hoping for a big piece of the fresh, warm bread.

LITTLE RED HEN	Now who will help me eat this bread?
DOG	I will.
CAT	Me too.
DUCK	So will I.
LITTLE RED HEN	Oh, no. No, you won't. Not you. Not you. Not you. None of you will eat this bread. I'm going to eat it myself.
NARRATOR	And she did. And that was the story of the Little Red Hen who worked very hard from nine to ten. No one helped the Little Red Hen. She did it all by herself.

RUMPELSTILTSKIN

NARRATOR
FATHER
DAUGHTER
KING
RUMPELSTILTSKIN
MESSENGER
QUEEN
CHORUS

NARRATOR
Once upon a time there was a poor working man who was very proud of his daughter. She was a pretty child, but her father thought she was the most beautiful child in the world. She was smart, but her father thought she was the smartest child in the world. She was sweet and nice and kind and good, but her father thought she was the sweetest, nicest, kindest, and best child in the whole wide world. The man loved to talk about all the wonderful things his daughter could do.

FATHER
She can swim like a fish.
She can sing like a bird.

82

She can do anything.
Yes, she can.
She can bake a cake.
She can speak Chinese.
She can do anything.
Yes, she can.
And, she can spin straw into gold!

CHORUS   What? What did you say?

FATHER   She can spin straw into gold!

CHORUS   Wow!
Did you hear that?
We must tell the King.
Straw into gold!
What a wonderful thing.
Straw into gold!
We must tell the King.
We must tell the King.
What a wonderful thing.

NARRATOR   When the King heard that there was
a girl who could spin straw into gold,
he sent for her father immediately.

KING   I heard you have a daughter.

FATHER	Yes, I do. A wonderful girl.
KING	I have heard many things about her.
FATHER	Yes, my daughter is a wonderful girl.
KING	I have heard that she can do many things. Many unusual things.
FATHER	Yes, she can, she can. She can swim like a fish. She can speak Chinese . . .
KING (in a whisper)	Yes, yes, so I've heard. But she can do other things, unusual things. I hear she spins straw into gold.
FATHER	Umm . . .
KING	Well?
FATHER	Umm . . .
KING	Does she or doesn't she?
FATHER	Umm . . . Umm . . .
KING	Is it really true? Can she do such a thing? Can she really spin straw into gold?
FATHER	Well, yes, of course, of course she can.
KING	Then bring her here. I must see for myself if she can spin straw into gold.

84

NARRATOR	And so the father went home, and told his daughter that the King wanted to meet her.
DAUGHTER	The King, the King? He wants to meet me? Why? Why?
FATHER	He wants to hear you sing.
DAUGHTER	What? Me? Sing? Sing for the King? How can I sing for the King? What can I sing? How can I sing for the King?
CHORUS	The King wants to see for himself, if she can spin straw into gold. Spin not sing, spin not sing. If she can spin straw into gold.

FATHER	Just go, my dear, and sing for the King. Go and sing for the King.
NARRATOR	And so the father took his daughter to the palace, and together they waited for the King.
KING	So you are the girl who spins straw into gold!
DAUGHTER	"Straw Into Gold," is that a new song? I don't sing "Straw Into Gold."
KING	I didn't say sing, I said spin, spin. I hear you spin straw into gold.
DAUGHTER	Straw into gold? Who told you that? I can't spin straw into gold. Tell him, Father, tell him please. I can't spin straw into gold.
CHORUS	Tell him, Father, tell him please. She can't spin straw into gold.
FATHER	Do the best you can, my child. Do the best you can.
NARRATOR	So the King took the poor girl to a small dark room. She looked around and saw nothing but straw and a spinning wheel.
KING	Here is the straw, and there is the wheel. You must spin the straw into gold!

DAUGHTER   But, I can't.
                    I can't spin straw into gold.

KING   You must try.
                    If you can't,
                    you will die.

CHORUS   If you can't,
                    you will die.
                    If you can't,
                    you will die.
                    You must try.
                    You must try.
                    If you can't,
                    you will die.

DAUGHTER   What am I going to do?
                    I can't spin straw into gold.
                    Oh, someone, somewhere,
                    help me please!
                    I can't spin straw into gold.

CHORUS   Someone, somewhere,
                    help her please!
                    She can't spin straw into gold.

NARRATOR   The girl sat down on the floor and began to cry. Suddenly, the door opened, and in danced a tiny little man. He was dressed all in silver from head to toe. His silver stockings and silver shoes sparkled when he moved. He spoke to the girl in a friendly voice.

RUMPELSTILTSKIN   Hi! Don't cry.

DAUGHTER   What? Who are you?

RUMPELSTILTSKIN   It doesn't matter who I am.
But who are you?
Why are you crying?

DAUGHTER   I'm just a simple country girl,
but I must spin straw into gold
or tomorrow I will die.

RUMPELSTILTSKIN   Straw into gold
or tomorrow you die?
Who told you that?

DAUGHTER   The King.

RUMPELSTILTSKIN   I see.
But what will you
do for me,
if I do this for you?

DAUGHTER   You can spin straw into gold?

RUMPELSTILTSKIN   Of course.
But what will you do for me?

DAUGHTER   Oh, let's see.
What can I give you?
Here, my necklace.
Take my necklace.

NARRATOR   He took her necklace, put it in his
pocket, sat down, and began to spin.
The sound of the spinning wheel
was so sweet, she fell asleep and
didn't wake up until the morning.
When she opened her eyes, the tiny
man was gone and the room was full
of gold. Then the door opened and,
the King came in.

KING	Straw into gold. Straw into gold. What a beautiful thing you have done for the King. Whatever you're doing, you must do it again.
DAUGHTER	Oh, no. Please! You don't understand. I can't spin straw into gold.
CHORUS	Oh, no. Please! You don't understand. She can't spin straw into gold.
KING	You did it once. You can do it again . . . By tomorrow or you die.
NARRATOR	So the King took the girl to a large room filled with straw, locked the door, and left. She looked around at the piles of straw, sat down, and began to cry.
DAUGHTER	What am I going to do? I can't spin straw into gold. Please little man, whoever you are, come back and help me, please.
NARRATOR	In a moment he was there, bouncing around the room like a tiny silver ball.
RUMPELSTILTSKIN	Hi! Don't cry. I'll help you. But what will you do for me?

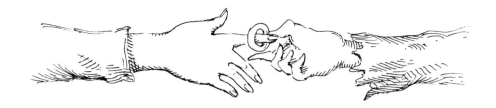

DAUGHTER	Oh, let's see. What can I give you? Here, my ring. Take my ring.
NARRATOR	And he took her ring, put it on his finger, sat down, and began to spin. The sound of the spinning wheel was so sweet, she fell asleep and didn't wake up until the morning. When she opened her eyes, the tiny man was gone, and the room was full of gold. Then the door opened, and the King came in.
KING	You've done it again! I've never seen such a thing in my life. Do it again, and I'll make you my wife.
DAUGHTER	Your wife?
KING	Yes, for the rest of your life. You will be Queen.
DAUGHTER	If you only knew. If you only knew.
KING	I know you can do it. You did it once. I know you can do it again.

CHORUS	Oh, no. Please! You don't understand. She can't spin straw into gold.
NARRATOR	And so for the third time, the King took the girl to a room even larger than before, and left her with a mountain of straw. She looked in every corner, hoping to find her friend.
DAUGHTER	Come out, come out, wherever you are. Whoever you are I need you now. Come back, come back, wherever you are. I need you now. Come back!
NARRATOR	In a moment he was there bouncing around the room once again.
DAUGHTER	Please, dear man. Can you do it again? Just one more time, and I'll be Queen.
RUMPELSTILTSKIN	You'll be Queen! I see. But what will you do for me?
DAUGHTER	I gave you my necklace. I gave you my ring. I have nothing left to give you now, but when I am Queen . . .
RUMPELSTILTSKIN	Yes? Yes? What will I get when you are Queen?

92

DAUGHTER	Anything!
RUMPELSTILTSKIN	Anything?
DAUGHTER	Gold, silver, diamonds, pearls.
RUMPELSTILTSKIN	Keep your diamonds. Keep your pearls. I will take your firstborn child.
DAUGHTER	Take my child? My firstborn child?
RUMPELSTILTSKIN	Yes, your child. I want your child.
DAUGHTER	My child? Never! Never! No!
RUMPELSTILTSKIN	If your answer is no, then I will go.

DAUGHTER	Oh, no. Don't go. All right, you win. You'll have my child. All right, you win. Don't go.
NARRATOR	For the third time, the tiny man sat down and began to spin. The sound of the wheel was so sweet, she fell asleep. When she woke up, the King was standing near her, and the room was full of gold.
KING	Wake up, my dear. You're going to be Queen. Wake up. You're going to be Queen.
NARRATOR	And so the girl married the King, and soon forgot all about her terrible promise. After a year, they had a beautiful daughter. Then one day when the Queen was in the nursery, the door opened.
CHORUS	Your firstborn child. Your firstborn child. He wants your firstborn child.
RUMPELSTILTSKIN	Where is the child? I have come for the child.
QUEEN	Oh, no. Not that! Take anything, but not my child.
RUMPELSTILTSKIN	You promised your child. I have come for the child.

QUEEN There must be something
else you need.
Something else you want . . .

RUMPELSTILTSKIN All right, if you like.
We can play a game,
but you'll have
only one chance.
You must guess my name.
You have three days,
or the child is mine.
Good-bye!

QUEEN Wait, don't go.
Guess your name?
What do you mean?
Guess your name?
How will I ever
guess your name?

RUMPELSTILTSKIN You have three days
to guess my name,
or the child is mine.
Good-bye!

NARRATOR The little man was gone in a puff of
silver smoke. The Queen was left
alone trying to think of all the names
she could starting with the letter A.

QUEEN Andy, Arnie,
Bobby, Billy,
Carlos, Charlie,
David, Dickie.

CHORUS You have three days
to guess his name.
Three days, three days.

QUEEN	Ernie, Eddie, Frankie, Freddie, Gary, Gerry, Herman, Harry.
NARRATOR	On the evening of the second day, the little man came and listened to the Queen guess his name. Finally, he said:
RUMPELSTILTSKIN	I'll give you a clue. It starts with R.
QUEEN	With R . . . with R? I must think of a name that starts with R. Let's see, is it Roger?
RUMPELSTILTSKIN	No.
QUEEN	Ralph?
RUMPELSTILTSKIN	No.
QUEEN	Richard? Robert? Randy?
RUMPELSTILTSKIN	No.
QUEEN	Raymond?
RUMPELSTILTSKIN	No.
QUEEN	Ronnie?
RUMPELSTILTSKIN	No.
QUEEN	Ricky?

RUMPELSTILTSKIN   NO, NO, NO, NO!

NARRATOR   And the second day ended with no more luck than the first. The Queen sent her messengers all over the land to search for clues to the name. On the afternoon of the third day, one of her messengers came running into the palace.

MESSENGER   The Queen, the Queen! I must see the Queen!

QUEEN   Quickly, what is it? Speak up, speak up.

MESSENGER   I was deep in the forest. I saw something there.

QUEEN   Quickly, quickly. What did you see?

MESSENGER   I heard something there.

QUEEN   What did you hear?

MESSENGER   I found something there.

QUEEN   What did you find?

MESSENGER   Deep in the forest I found a house. In front of the house I saw a fire. In front of the fire I saw, I saw . . .

QUEEN   Yes? Yes? What did you see?

MESSENGER   I saw a man, a tiny man. Dressed all in silver from head to toe. He said a word I've never heard.

QUEEN What was the word?

MESSENGER Rumpelstiltskin.
Over and over and over again.
Rumpelstiltskin, Rumpelstiltskin.

CHORUS Rumpelstiltskin.
Over and over and over again,
Rumpelstiltskin, Rumpelstiltskin.

NARRATOR So the messenger and the Queen
hurried to the forest, and hid near
the house. In front of the house a
fire was burning, and around the
fire a man was dancing, chanting
Rumpelstiltskin, Rumpelstiltskin.

QUEEN That's it! That's him!

RUMPELSTILTSKIN Today's the day!
Tonight's the night!
Tomorrow I'll take
the young Queen's child.
The child is mine.
I won the game.
Rumpelstiltskin
is my name.

QUEEN	Rumpelstiltskin is his name.
NARRATOR	And the Queen and her messenger hurried back to the palace to wait for Rumpelstiltskin.
RUMPELSTILTSKIN	Your time is up. I have come for the child. Or have you, ha, ha, guessed my name?
QUEEN	Guessed your name? There are so many names that start with R.
RUMPELSTILTSKIN	Of course there are, but I'll give you a clue. The first letter is R, the second is U.
CHORUS	The first is R. The second is U. R-U R-U
QUEEN	R-U-M-P E-L-S-T I-L-T-S K-I-N RUMPELSTILTSKIN!
RUMPELSTILTSKIN	What? How?
CHORUS	R-U-M-P-E-L-S-T-I-L-T-S-K-I-N RUMPELSTILTSKIN!
RUMPELSTILTSKIN	Oh, no! I lost the game! Yes, Rumpelstiltskin is my name.

NARRATOR   And with these words,
Rumpelstiltskin began to spin
around and around and around. He
fell to the ground in a cloud of silver
smoke. Only a tiny silver button
remained. The Queen and the
King lived happily ever after. And
when the Queen put her child to bed
at night, she would show her the tiny
silver button. Then she would tell
the child her favorite story—the
story of Rumpelstiltskin.

THE FISHERMAN
AND HIS WIFE

NARRATOR
THE FISHERMAN
THE FISHERMAN'S WIFE
THE FLOUNDER
CHORUS

NARRATOR

Once upon a time, a fisherman and his wife lived in a house by the sea. The fisherman loved to go out alone in his boat, and sit and fish, and wait for a bite from a fish at the bottom of the sea.

CHORUS

Sit and fish,
and wait for a bite.
Sit and fish,
and wait for a bite.
Sit and fish,
and wait for a bite
from a fish at
the bottom of the sea.

NARRATOR

One day he made up a song to sing to the fish while he waited.

FISHERMAN   (Melody: Twinkle, Twinkle Little Star)

Catfish, catfish,
starfish, too.
Tuna salad sandwich,
oyster stew.
Catfish heads and catfish tails.
Catfish fins and catfish scales.
Catfish, catfish,
starfish, too.
Tuna salad sandwich,
oyster stew.

NARRATOR   Sometimes, out there alone in the dark, the fisherman saw strange things. Once he saw the shadow of a mermaid's tail, and once he saw the terrible fish with four eyes, the one that brings bad luck. But the strangest night of all was the night he felt his fishing pole begin to shake, rattle, and roll.

FISHERMAN   Hey, what's this?
Oh, my! What's this?

NARRATOR	And he began to pull in his line very slowly and carefully. After a moment, he saw the head of a very big fish.
FISHERMAN	WOW! Look at that! What a fine fat fish! I've never seen such a thing in my life. I wonder what kind of fish it is?
FLOUNDER	I'm a flounder.
FISHERMAN	What? Did I hear something?
FLOUNDER	I said, I'm a flounder.
FISHERMAN	What? A talking fish?
FLOUNDER	Yes, a talking fish. Listen carefully. Listen carefully.
FISHERMAN	I'm listening. I'm listening.
FLOUNDER	I am a magic fish. Throw me back to the sea, and I will give you anything in the world you want.
FISHERMAN	What?
FLOUNDER	You heard what I said. Anything you want. Say the word, and it will be yours.
FISHERMAN	Anything?
FLOUNDER	Anything.

FISHERMAN	I can't believe it—a talking fish. A fish who will give me whatever I wish.
FLOUNDER	Throw me back and you will see.
FISHERMAN	What shall I do? Keep him or throw him back?
CHORUS ONE	Keep him, keep him. Take him home and eat him. Don't throw him back, no. Don't throw him back.
CHORUS TWO	Pick him up and throw him back. Pick him up and throw him back. Throw him back. Throw him back. Pick him up and throw him back. You'll be sorry if you keep him. Pick him up and throw him back.

NARRATOR　　The fisherman thought about it for a few moments. Then he picked up the flounder, and threw him back into the water. At first, the big fish swam right down to the bottom of the sea, but in a moment, he was back to keep his promise.

FLOUNDER　　Tell me what you want,
and it will be yours.

CHORUS　　Tell him, tell him.
Tell him what you want.
Tell him, tell him.
Tell him what you want.

FISHERMAN　　Hmmm, let's see.
What do I want?
What do I want?
I can't think of a thing.
I can't think of a thing.

CHORUS　　He can't think of a thing.
He can't think of a thing.

NARRATOR　　And then the flounder disappeared into the deep dark sea. The fisherman hurried home to tell his wife the story. When she heard him coming, she ran to the door but she was disappointed when she didn't see any fish.

WIFE　　Oh, no! Didn't you catch anything?

FISHERMAN　　I did! I caught a flounder.

WIFE	Well, where is it? What did you do with it?
FISHERMAN	I threw it back.
WIFE	You threw it back? Why? Why did you throw it back?
NARRATOR	So the fisherman sat down and told her the whole story. As she listened to him, her eyes got bigger and bigger. When he had finished, she said:
WIFE	Imagine that! A talking fish. I wish you'd asked for something.
FISHERMAN	Asked for what? Asked for what?
WIFE	Well, you could have asked for a house.

FISHERMAN	A house? But we have a house.
WIFE	Yes, but look how small it is. We need a bigger house.
FISHERMAN	Bigger than this?
WIFE	Yes, bigger than this.
FISHERMAN	How big? How many rooms?
WIFE	Let's see. Let's see. One for you and one for me. One for this and one for that. One for you and one for me. One, two, three, four.
FISHERMAN	Four rooms? Four rooms? What'll we do with four rooms?
CHORUS	Four rooms. Four rooms. What'll they do with four rooms?
WIFE	Four rooms, why four? Four rooms, why not more?
CHORUS	Why four? Why not more? Why four? Why not more?
WIFE	Why not five, six, or seven? Why not nine? Nine sounds fine.
FISHERMAN	Nine rooms? Nine rooms? What'll we do with nine rooms?
WIFE	I want a house with nine rooms. Why not nine? Nine sounds fine.

FISHERMAN	We're only two. What'll we do with nine rooms, nine rooms?
CHORUS	They're only two. What'll they do with nine big rooms? The fisherman's wife, The fisherman's wife, wants a house with nine rooms.
WIFE	Tell that flounder nine rooms!
FISHERMAN	Oh, oh! I don't know.
WIFE	Don't you worry. He can do it. Ask that fish for nine rooms.
NARRATOR	And so the fisherman went down to the edge of the sea, and called the flounder.
FISHERMAN	Flounder, flounder in the sea. Flounder, flounder come to me.
NARRATOR	Soon the flounder appeared.

FLOUNDER	Yes? What do you want?
FISHERMAN	Oh, flounder, flounder, it's not me. I don't want a thing, but my wife . . . She . . .
FLOUNDER	Yes? Tell me. What does she want?
FISHERMAN	She wants a house . . .
FLOUNDER	What kind of a house?
FISHERMAN	A big house.
FLOUNDER	How big? How many rooms?
FISHERMAN	Nine!
FLOUNDER	Nine rooms?
FISHERMAN	That's what she said. But if that's too hard for you to do . . .
FLOUNDER	The house is hers. Go home! Go home!
CHORUS	The house is hers. The house is hers. She has her house with nine rooms. Go home to the house with nine rooms. The house is hers. Go home.
NARRATOR	And so the fisherman thanked the flounder, and hurried home to his wife. There she was in her big house with nine rooms. For a while they

were very happy, but one day when the fisherman came home after working hard, his wife met him at the door. Her eyes were shining, and she said:

WIFE   Call the flounder.

FISHERMAN   Call the flounder? What for?

WIFE   I have an idea.

FISHERMAN   An idea? An idea?

WIFE   I want you to be King.

FISHERMAN   Me?

WIFE   Yes, you! I want you to be King.

FISHERMAN   That's the worst idea I've ever heard.
I don't want to be King.

WIFE   Then I'll be King.
I'll be King.
If you won't, I will.
I'll be King.

CHORUS   She'll be King.
She'll be King.
If he won't, she will.
She'll be King.

WIFE   Call the fish.
Call the fish.
Tell him I want to be King.

FISHERMAN   How can I ask for a thing like that?

WIFE   I hate the life
of a fisherman's wife.
I want to be King.
I have to be King.
I must be King.
I will be King.

CHORUS   She wants to be King.
She has to be King.
She must be King.
She will be King.

WIFE   I hate the life
of a fisherman's wife.
Tell him I want to be King.
Go to the flounder.
Go now.
Tell him I want to be King.

NARRATOR	And so the fisherman went down to the sea, and called the flounder.
FISHERMAN	Flounder, flounder in the sea. Flounder, flounder come to me.
NARRATOR	Soon the flounder appeared, and the fisherman told him that his wife wanted to be King.
FLOUNDER	Go home, my friend. Your wife is King.
NARRATOR	And so the fisherman went home, but he didn't see his house. Instead of his house, he saw a castle, and his wife was sitting inside wearing a crown.
CHORUS	The fisherman's wife is wearing a crown. The fisherman's wife. The fisherman's wife. The fisherman's wife is wearing a crown. The fisherman's wife is King.
NARRATOR	And so the fisherman and his wife, the King, lived together happily in the castle for a while, but one morning . . .

WIFE	Wake up! Wake up! I have an idea!
FISHERMAN	Oh, no! What is it now?
WIFE	Go to the flounder. Tell him please. I'm tired of being the King. Everyday, the same old thing. I'm tired of being the King. Tired and bored. Nothing to do. I hate the life of a King. I hate the life of a fisherman's wife. But I'm tired of being the King.
CHORUS	Tired and bored. Nothing to do. Everyday, the same old thing. She hates the life of a fisherman's wife. But she's tired of being the King.

FISHERMAN	But what shall I say? What do you want?
WIFE	Tell him I want something better than this. Bigger and better. Bigger and better.
CHORUS	Bigger and better. Bigger and better. Bigger and better than this.
FISHERMAN	Bigger and better than this? What could be bigger and better than this?
WIFE	Tell him I want to be Emperor.
FISHERMAN	Emperor? Oh, no!
WIFE	Go. Go to the flounder now.
FISHERMAN	How? How can I ask such a thing?
WIFE	I am the King. Go. Go to the flounder now.
NARRATOR	And so the fisherman went back to the sea, and for the third time called the flounder.
FISHERMAN	Flounder, flounder in the sea. Flounder, flounder come to me.
NARRATOR	Just as before, the flounder appeared, and spoke in a friendly voice.
FLOUNDER	Yes? What is it?

NARRATOR	And the fisherman told the flounder that his wife wanted to be Emperor.
FLOUNDER	Go home, my friend. Your wife is the Emperor.
NARRATOR	And with a sigh, the flounder disappeared into the water. The fisherman went home to his wife, the Emperor, and together they lived happily for a while. But one morning . . .
WIFE	Wake up! Wake up! I have an idea.
FISHERMAN	Oh, no! What is it now?
WIFE	Listen to me carefully. I want to make the stars shine. Look at the sun. Look at the sky. I want to make the sun rise. I want to make the sun rise and set. I want to make the stars shine.
CHORUS	She wants to make the sun rise and set. She wants to make the stars shine.
FISHERMAN	Oh, no! Oh, no!
WIFE	I want to make the snow.
FISHERMAN	Oh, no!

WIFE	Go to the flounder now, go! Tell him I want to make the snow. Tell him I want to make the sun rise and the sky turn red, and the moon come out. Tell him I want to make the stars shine. Tell him I want to make the snow.
CHORUS	Tell him what she wants. Tell him what she wants. Tell him she wants to make the stars shine. Tell him she wants to make the snow.
FISHERMAN	No, I can't. No, no, I can't.
WIFE	Go. Go to the flounder, now.
FISHERMAN	How? How can I ask such a thing?
WIFE	I am the Emperor. Go. Go to the flounder now.

NARRATOR	And so once again, the fisherman went down to the sea, took a very deep breath, and sadly called the flounder.
FISHERMAN	Flounder, flounder in the sea. Flounder, flounder come to me.
NARRATOR	Soon the flounder appeared and said:

FLOUNDER	Yes? What is it?
FISHERMAN	I hate to ask you this, but . . .
FLOUNDER	Yes? What is it?
FISHERMAN	It's my wife, the Emperor.
FLOUNDER	Yes? What does the Emperor want?
FISHERMAN	She wants . . . She wants . . .
FLOUNDER	Speak up! Speak up! What does she want?

FISHERMAN	She wants to make the sun rise. And the stars come out.
FLOUNDER	What are you saying?
FISHERMAN	She wants to make the sky turn red. And the rain fall. And the snow . . .
FLOUNDER	Stop it! Stop it! I've heard enough.
CHORUS	Stop it! Stop it! Enough's enough. Stop it! Stop it! Now!
NARRATOR	As the flounder spoke, there was lightning and thunder in the sky. The wind blew over the dark water, and for a moment, the flounder disappeared under a very big wave. But then suddenly, he returned and spoke to the fisherman for the last time.
FLOUNDER	Listen to me carefully. The answer is no. The answer is no. The stars? The moon? The rain? The snow? The sun? The sky? The answer is NO!
CHORUS	The answer is no. The stars? The moon? The rain? The snow? The answer is NO!

NARRATOR

And then the flounder disappeared into the angry sea. The fisherman went home, and found that all of the things the flounder had given them were gone. They were back where they had started, in their simple house. As time passed, the fisherman almost forgot the story. He didn't miss the big house, or the time when his wife was the King. But sometimes at night when the moon was full, and he thought he saw the shadow of a mermaid's tail, he missed the sound of the flounder, and he would call out his name not to ask for anything, just to see him, and hear that beautiful voice.

FISHERMAN

Flounder, flounder in the sea.
Flounder, flounder come to me.

NARRATOR

But he never did, and no one ever saw him again.